W9-ATN-514

PRAISE

"For me, this series is like a gift... It takes you on a journey."
—Actor Pierre Arditi, who stars in the TV series

"Difficult to forget and oddly addictive... deserves a high mark for keeping the answers hidden and the pages turning."
—*ForeWord Reviews*

"Another clever and highly entertaining mystery by an incredibly creative writing duo, never disappointing, always marvelously atypical."
—*Unshelfish*

"It is full of intrigue and deceit, and it kept me turning pages and guessing. A very pleasant and enticing read, with a few epicurean suggestions."
—*Books Chatter*

"This is a fun and informative take on the cozy crime mystery, French style."
—*Eurocrime*

"This is is a quick, pleasant read, a good introduction to the country's culinary charms and regional beauty."
—*Crime Fiction Lover*

"You'll travel to France to taste the complex flavors, the unraveling of a mystery, while relishing the French countryside, the gourmet dishes, and the simple pleasurable delight of this rare series."

—5-star educator review

"A smooth, jubilatory discovery of French wine country. I love these."

—5-star reader review

"A good vintage with tasty dialogue and a solid plot."

—*Tele-loisir*

"A fine vintage."

—Award-winning mystery writer Peter May

Flambé in Armagnac

A Winemaker Detective Mystery

Jean-Pierre Alaux
and
Noël Balen

Translated by Sally Pane

LE FRENCH BOOK ▮

First published in France as
Question d'eaux-de-vie...ou de mort
by Jean-Pierre Alaux and Noël Balen

World copyright ©Librairie Arthème Fayard, 2004

English translation copyright ©2015 Sally Pane

First published in English in 2015
By Le French Book, Inc., New York

www.lefrenchbook.com

Translator: Sally Pane
Translation editor: Amy Richard
Proofreader: Chris Gage
Cover designer: Jeroen ten Berge

ISBN:
Trade paperback: 9781939474414
E-book: 9781939474421
Hardback: 9781939474438

Inhale the scent of split oak trees our barrels are made of. They smell of damp earth and marauding herds, a sort of musky odor, from which the eau-de-vie, after four or five years in the cask, forever retains a wild perfume.

—Joseph de Pesquidoux

1

A hot-air balloon was slipping into the clouds above a herd of wild horses. A village of rustic chalets hewn from rough logs stood silently on a ridge against a blue sky. Naiads in Brazilian bikinis frolicked beneath a blue waterfall. Swans in a Japanese-style pond navigated around pastel water lilies and gleaming orange koi.

"Which calendar would you like, Mr. Cooker?" Angèle was standing on the doorstep, stamping her feet and wrapped in a blue and yellow coat bearing the postal service insignia. Benjamin Cooker studied the images, where eternal peace reigned on earth and life was so simple and innocent. He pretended to hesitate between one filled with sandy beaches and rolling surf and another featuring nostalgic side streets in Caribbean locales. He finally chose the dog calendar, with an Irish setter that looked like a younger version of his canine companion Bacchus.

Once a year, Angèle rang the doorbells on her delivery route, not for the mail, but to sell calendars. It was a holiday ritual postal service workers in France shared with street cleaners and firefighters. Benjamin always bought one from each group, occasionally wondering what the money went for. Perhaps it was for an end-of-year bonus or for widows and orphans. Of course he never asked. That wouldn't do, not with a tradition nearly as old as the postal service itself.

Benjamin offered the woman a cup of tea, but quickly added, "Or a cup of coffee?"

"Frankly, I'd prefer that!"

"One sugar?"

"Two, if you please. And how is Mrs. Cooker?"

"Well. Very well, indeed! She's preparing for our daughter Margaux's impending arrival—out shopping in Bordeaux. This visit is a real treat for us. It's not often that Margaux tears herself away from New York these days. At any rate, I do hope Mrs. Cooker doesn't go overboard, or I may not want to open our next credit-card statement!"

"How you do go on, Mr. Cooker. You of all people know that wine is made to be drunk. It's the same with money; it's made to be spent. Don't you agree?"

The renowned wine consultant and author of the bestselling *Cooker Guide* wasn't sure he wanted to engage in a discussion that he knew he couldn't win. So he walked over to the mantel to pick up the envelope he had prepared. Angèle was all smiles.

"Happy New Year, Mr. Cooker!" Angèle said, leaning in for good-bye cheek kisses. Two pecks, one on each side, was standard in the Bordeaux region. It was three in southeastern France and four farther north.

The winemaker was hardly a fan of such effusion. Angèle's kisses, however, were something no healthy man could refuse. The young woman's cheeks were pink from a morning spent in the cold, and her chestnut hair smelled of coffee.

Benjamin watched from the warmth of Grangebelle as the mail carrier's van disappeared down the drive. The weather was cold enough to chill Champagne, and some of the elderly residents of Saint-Julien were fearfully recalling the winter of 1954, although, on average, temperatures this winter had been warmer than usual. Benjamin had decided against going to his office on the Allées de Tourny. It felt good to be at Grangebelle, quietly watching the flames in the fireplace. The scent of the burning wood mingled with the slightly bitter smell of cigar.

The winemaker poured himself another cup of tea before perusing his mail a bit wearily. Bacchus was dozing on the old Persian rug in front of the fire. This was the dog's favorite pastime in the winter. When the temperature dropped, Benjamin had a hard time rousing him for the long walks they usually loved to take. The old dog would not budge.

3

In the bundle of mail, one envelope caught his attention. In black and red letters, it bore the name Protection Insurance. Cooker & Co. occasionally did work for this company, and Benjamin always wound up chastising himself for not charging more, considering the time the cases took. Judging from the impersonal form letters they always sent, they clearly didn't know him from Adam. In all of southwest France, he was the sole wine expert whose testimony was accepted without question by the courts in Toulouse and Bordeaux. He drew deeply on his Havana and put on his reading glasses.

Protection Insurance
Building Pierre-Paul-de-Riquet, C3
Quartier Compans-Caffarelli
31026 Toulouse Cedex

Dear Sir,
Pursuant to claim No. 455/JV/40, we are pleased to appoint you to estimate the damages suffered by our client, Mr. Jean-Charles de Castayrac, as a result of an accidental fire that destroyed the wine cellar on his property, Château Blanzac in Labastide-d'Armagnac, on December 24.
Your assignment is to provide a precise determination of the Armagnac reserves stored in the claimant's cellar preceding the fire, to assess the quality of his eau-de-vie products up until that

*time, to estimate Mr. Castayrac's loss, based on the
market value of the Armagnac, and to examine Mr.
Castayrac's records.*

*Your expert report must be sent to our company
headquarters within thirty days. It is your respon-
sibility to investigate this matter with the diligence
and skill you have always exercised and for which
our company is grateful.*

Sincerely,
Étienne Valéry
Manager, Claims Investigation

Benjamin considered turning down the assignment. But then he realized that the job would be
an excellent excuse to pay a visit to his old friend
Philippe de Bouglon. The fact that they had not
been in touch for months did not diminish their
friendship. And besides, his reserves of Armagnac
were running low, and it was high time to replen-
ish the liquor cabinet at Grangebelle.

Just a month earlier, in fact, Elisabeth and
he had taken a drive through Labastide, hoping
to visit the Bouglons and buy some Armagnac.
Unfortunately, Philippe and his wife, Beatrice,
had been away on vacation, but in town they
had come across Francisco, the cellar master at
Château Blanzac. He apologized for not being
able to accommodate them immediately, but had
promised to personally deliver some of the highly

regarded eau-de-vie that he planned to distill before the holidays. Elisabeth had assured Francisco that they could wait.

"I didn't know the Blanzac cellar master was so charming," Elisabeth had remarked, a smile on her face as she watched the man hurry off.

"Oh yes, as appealing as his Armagnac," Benjamin had said with a bit of a grumble.

Had any of Château Blanzac's fine Armagnac survived the fire? He'd find out. At any rate, Benjamin would catch the Bouglons at home. He decided not to call ahead. He would simply show up unannounced. After all, the Bouglons were two of the most hospitable people he knew. So the New Year was getting off to a good start. The winemaker threw another log on the fire. Bacchus just yawned and closed his eyes again. Benjamin savored another puff of his morning cigar. It was beginning to taste exquisite. What a pity the teapot was empty.

Benjamin opened the door to feel the chill on his face. The outdoor thermometer read six degrees below zero. The Gironde River and the fields of the Médoc, all speckled in white, seemed to be reaching toward the patches of pale sunshine from heaven. He did prefer the cold to the rain, but driving on ice was not his favorite sport. At any rate, Virgile, his assistant, would take the wheel.

Benjamin closed the door and headed to the phone.

"Hello, Virgile? Cooker here. Happy New Year, my boy! Let's celebrate with a glass of Armagnac. What do you say? Meet me at Grangebelle. And bring along some warm clothes and your toothbrush."

Benjamin quickly scribbled a note for Elisabeth telling her where he'd be and went into his bedroom to fetch his own toothbrush and an overnight bag.

2

The heavy wrought-iron gate was open at Château Prada. Virgile drove Benjamin's convertible into the huge courtyard, and the winemaker spotted someone pushing aside the lace curtain at one of the small windows in the kitchen. He thought he recognized the profile of his friend, with his inimitable heavy moustache.

Benjamin watched as his assistant who had never been here, took in the enormous complex. The château's elegant grandeur and perfect symmetry spoke volumes for the Bouglons' past fortune. The outbuildings on either side of the central building attested to the agricultural enterprise of the property. Even in the midst of a glacial winter, Prada symbolized the steadfast provincial aristocracy that had never failed the king of France.

"Look at the chimney, Virgile. Our timing is impeccable!"

"How can you say that, boss, when you didn't even have the courtesy to tell your friends we were coming?"

Benjamin hastily pulled on his Loden, as he assessed his assistant's fatigue after two hours of driving on winding roads covered with ice. The young man looked his usual handsome, athletic self.

"It's an old trick of country priests, Virgile. Back in the day, when clergy called on the nobles of a parish, the priest would look up at the chimneys of the best châteaus. If smoke was rising straight to the sky, he would continue on his way. But if plumes of smoke were escaping in little puffs, he didn't hesitate to knock. He was sure to share in some perfectly prepared feast."

"And why was that?" Virgile asked.

"Think, Virgile! Because then he knew that a simmering pot was hanging from the rack."

"Whatever you say, boss."

Before Benjamin could give Virgile a disapproving look, Philippe de Bouglon was on the doorstep, hands on his hips and a grin on his ruddy face, true Gascon that he was.

"Benjamin! What polar wind has brought you to us? Your reserves of Armagnac must really be running dry for you to come to Labastide in weather like this! Or did Elisabeth kick you out? Don't tell me you've already had lunch, or I'll be offended."

Beatrice appeared behind her husband, radiant in a sky-blue turtleneck and cream-colored velvet slacks. Her eyes were bright, and her voice was deep and warm. They wished one another a happy New Year. Benjamin introduced Virgile, telling the Bouglons that he was talented in the art of blending but something of a novice when it came to Armagnac.

"You've come at just the right time, Benjamin," Beatrice said.

The winemaker watched as she exchanged a look of complicity with her husband.

"Guess what's on today's menu," she continued.

"Don't tell me you've cooked the farmyard ducks," Benjamin ventured.

"No, even better!"

The winemaker lifted his nose to sniff the aromas coming from the kitchen.

"Pan-seared foie gras, perhaps?"

"If you ask me, I'd say squab, in a stew, perhaps a traditional salmis," Virgile said.

"I would be worried if I were you, Benjamin. He has a keen nose. Your charming assistant is right. He might just steal your reputation one day."

"That will be a proud day for me," Benjamin said.

"You did get the foie gras right, though," Beatrice said. "I roasted the bird and reduced the drippings with Armagnac, before adding some foie gras. Now the bird's cut up and reheating in the sauce. You're right on time."

"Knowing you, it's wood pigeon. Someone's been out hunting again. Wonderful. You know how fond I am of game birds. We haven't had any at home since I gave up hunting and sent Bacchus into early retirement."

Château Prada's owner related his story of hunting the previous day in the Mézin forest bordering the Gers and Lot-et-Garonne. Philippe and his companions had spent the entire morning in their lookouts, shivering to the bone, gobbling snacks, and overindulging in Armagnac and coffee. For two years now, the migratory birds had proved to be as capricious as they were rare. It was said that their flight corridors had moved to the west for some unknown reason. Ringdoves coming from eastern countries were following the coastline along the Bay of Biscay. Other less adventurous birds were spreading out over the cornfields between Adour and Garonne. The wood pigeons Philippe had bagged belonged to the hungry breed that preferred to hold out rather than take a chance. The hunter from Labastide was quite proud of his booty: four specimens with blue-gray plumage and bloodred beaks.

"It was freezing."

"But you were rewarded for your patience, which—you'd admit—isn't your strongest virtue."

"That's a low blow, Benjamin. But I will be a gentleman and extend a heartfelt invitation to this feast, prepared by the best chef in Gascony. I should know. I married her, and I thank God for every day that I spend with her."

"Let's not go overboard," Beatrice said, pushing back a lock of blond hair from her high forehead.

Philippe de Bouglon smoothed his moustache. "What about a Folle d'Armagnac as an aperitif? How does that sound? I just need to add two place settings to the table and run to the cellar so that we can honor the presence of the most famous winemaker in France. Excuse me—in Europe. I mean the world! I will be right with you, gentlemen."

Checking the grandfather clock, Beatrice excused herself. The chef could not abandon the stew. Benjamin and Virgile took the opportunity to study the Bouglon portrait gallery. Some of Philippe's forebears had distinguished themselves in far-off battles, and others had planted the vineyard at a time when Armagnac was shipped along the Baïse and Garonne rivers to Bordeaux. From there it was sent all over Europe.

A grand piano took up a large portion of the living room. Benjamin watched as Virgile started to slide his fingers across the ivory keys but thought better of it and stopped. Instead, he gazed out at the garden, where a few Lebanon cedars broke the monotony of the frost-covered lawn. The small living room was damp. The marble floor and fixtures, which dominated the room, reinforced the sense of cold. Virgile was visibly chilled—most likely hungry too. He had pulled up his collar. Benjamin felt the same urge, but he didn't want to embarrass his gracious hosts. If only Philippe would hurry back with his Armagnac.

Seconds later, Philippe de Bouglon walked through the doorway, bottle in hand. The transparent Folle d'Armagnac resembled the purest vodka. A mischievous glint shone in the bright eyes of the master of the house. Benjamin, noticing his assistant rubbing his chin in bewilderment, came to his rescue.

"Virgile, did your professors at wine school skip over Folle d'Armagnac? If so, they should be hanged!"

"I have a vague memory of something. They did talk to us about Blanche d'Armagnac, I think."

"It's the same thing, Virgile. It's not to be confused with folle-blanche, the grape variety."

"Yes, now I remember. It was a fatal mistake on my part, made on a written exam. My professor treated me like an idiot. 'You are about as qualified to work in wine as I am to give sermons at Notre Dame,' he said."

"Well he misread you, didn't he?" Benjamin said, extending his glass to the flask proffered by his friend Philippe.

Philippe was grinning. Even before they sipped this Blanche d'Armagnac of his, it had the power to prompt discussion and curiosity. Wasn't that the very characteristic of wine? The French politician and diplomat Tallyrand had said this—more pompously—some two hundred years earlier.

"It's barely out of the still, clear, white, untouched by wood, never aged, so never sipped by angels," Philippe explained. "If you would allow me a comparison, Benjamin, this eau-de-vie is our virgin of sorts. It's all pureness—and finesse. Taste it! You perceive floral notes of... How shall I put it?"

"You can already smell the fruit," Virgile began to say.

"Philippe, please don't use the word 'virgin' around this skirt-chaser I have for an assistant. He's likely to find qualities in your Armagnac that don't exist."

"Well, this young man must be Gascon. Are you?"

"Actually, I am, on my maternal grandmother's side. She was from Lectoure."

"I knew it," Bouglon said.

By the time they were ready to eat, Benjamin was no longer chilled. The Blanche d'Armagnac had produced the desired effect, warming the mind and the body.

They dined in the kitchen, which was warmer than the dining room. Old grapevine stocks fueled the kitchen fireplace, and the thick glowing embers promised a perfectly cooked stew. The room was filled with wonderful aromas. Enchanting frost crystals had formed around the leaded windows overlooking the estate's pollarded plane trees. The water pipes had frozen, and the faucet was no longer working, but who cared? At Prada, one was hardly inclined to drink water.

Beatrice brought out one of her vintage jars of duck foie gras, appropriately truffled. A 1989 Suduiraut Cuvée Madame, exquisitely amber in color, accompanied the feast.

Benjamin was relishing his visit with Philippe. The two happily recalled the old days when they were still bachelors. The sauterne had served to re-kindle their ribald memories. Virgile, meanwhile, responded politely to the stream of questions from the mistress of Prada.

"Beatrice, I'm afraid you're going to embarrass our friend with your interrogation," Philippe said, turning to his wife and putting down his fork.

There was no hint of reproach in his tone. Indeed, Benjamin thought he detected a loving intimacy in his smile.

"Oh Philippe, Virgile and I have already become friends. I've found out a lot of things, beginning with the reason for our dear friend Benjamin's visit to Labastide. They're here about the fire at Château Blanzac. It's all anybody is talking about around here."

"Yes, it's horrible," Philippe responded. "You wouldn't wish that on anyone, not even your worst enemy."

Benjamin pierced a piece of bread with his fork and dipped it in the enticing sauce on his plate. "Would you count this Jean-Claude de Castayrac among your friends, Philippe?" he asked before bringing the fork to his mouth.

"He's neither a friend nor an enemy, Benjamin. We know each other well. I even have a certain respect for him. But to be frank, I prefer his Armagnac to his company."

"Can you be more specific?"

Philippe de Bouglon's reddish moustache was beginning to glisten with the stew juices. The Château Pavie he had brought to room temperature by the fireplace had put a gleam in his gray eyes. Before Philippe could satisfy Benjamin's curiosity, Beatrice answered for him.

"You know, everyone here looks out for himself. The producers respect each other, and sometimes we exchange samples. But basically, we see one another at the Armagnac Promotion Committee meetings and competitions at Eauze and Aire-sur-l'Adour. That's about it. As far as the fire goes, the one to feel sorry for isn't Castayrac. He'll always make out okay. It's poor Vasquez! Dying like that in the fire. It's terrible. They say the still exploded. I hope he didn't suffer."

"You mean Francisco, the cellar master? That's terrible. There was no mention of a death in the letter from the insurance company." Benjamin was shocked. How had he missed this piece of news?

17

Philippe wiped his mouth with his sauce-stained napkin. He picked up the bottle of Saint-Émilion and filled his guests' empty glasses. "One thing is certain: Francisco was the only one who made the baron's Armagnacs. His sons had no say in the matter. Castayrac trusted his cellar master, and he did a good job. Francisco's brandies are among the best in Bas-Armagnac."

"Better than yours?" Virgile ventured.

Philippe was unequivocal. "To you, I can admit the truth. Yes, I am—that is, I *was*—envious of Château Blanzac's Armagnacs. They have an elegance, a finesse. You understand, don't you, Benjamin?"

Benjamin was distracted. He was still thinking about Francisco's tragic death. He pulled himself together and listened to his friend. He was touched by Philippe's candor and admiration. In truth, Benjamin had never tasted Blanzac's brandies, although he had been looking forward to it after his unexpected encounter with Francisco a month earlier. And to think he would have to evaluate the exact worth of the château's reserves.

"I've heard that his paradise was full to the roof," Benjamin confided, referring to the warehouse where he stored his vintages. "At least that's what he told the insurance company."

"Old Castayrac definitely had reserves," Philippe said, offering Benjamin the cheese platter. "These days, everyone has reserves. Unfortunately,

Armagnac isn't selling as well as we'd like. It doesn't matter whether the Armagnac's good or bad. We're all stuck with barrels up to the ceiling and no one to drink what's in them, except the angels. I just wish the angels could pay my bills."

"Yes, but I've been under the impression that your Armagnac is doing well. I see it everywhere. I was in London two weeks ago, on Saint James Street, and I shared one of your brandies with an old friend."

"Don't kid yourself, Benjamin. I have enough in my cellar to supply the French Senate for a century. In both Cognac and Armagnac, we've all got problems, and our government isn't helping."

Beatrice had left the table and returned with a sumptuous-looking pumpkin cake that was giving off the subtle scent of cinnamon. Benjamin and Virgile clapped in unison.

"Beatrice, once again you've outdone yourself," Philippe said, giving his wife a wink.

The master of the house rose to fan the hearth. He threw a worm-eaten black-oak log on the embers, and flames immediately rose from the wood.

"A good Armagnac can only be appreciated around a hearth," Philippe said. "How about a 1983 Prada?"

Virgile nodded in agreement, but Benjamin quickly put his hand on his arm.

"No offense, Philippe, but I'd like to taste a brandy from Château Blanzac. I'm sure you have that on hand. Just to help me form an opinion."

Benjamin detected the hint of a frown on his affable friend's face. "I'm afraid I'm all out. I would gladly have…"

Then his wife betrayed him with her typical spontaneity. "Philippe, go look in Grandmother's display cabinet. I think there's a bottle that Francisco brought us. Remember it, dear? For your fiftieth birthday."

"What would I do without you?" Philippe sighed. His ruse had fooled no one.

Benjamin was taking two cigars in silky wrappers from his leather case when Philippe disappeared behind the double doors to the office. He knew his friend was a big fan of Havanas. The Cubans guaranteed an hour of sheer pleasure. No doubt Jean-Charles de Castayrac's Armagnac would make the occasion even more memorable.

He was about to imagine them raising a glass to the deceased cellar master when an ear-piercing crack pulled him out of his musings. Beatrice, Virgile, and Benjamin ran to the window. A peach tree had snapped under the weight of the ice. The winemaker glanced at Beatrice and saw that she was shivering.

No sooner had they absorbed the sight of the felled peach tree than the sound of breaking glass rang out behind the door. "Damn it all!"

"Oh, that doesn't sound good," Beatrice said, pushing back the lock of blond hair that seemed to have a mind of its own.

When Philippe opened the door, the exquisite fragrances of honey, pear, and orange preserves wafted into the kitchen. A long silence ensued.

In a cloud of smoke, Benjamin finally looked Philippe de Bouglon in the eye. "Now I know why you were envious of Lord de Castayrac's Armagnacs. And if you weren't my friend, I'd almost suspect you of having broken the bottle to avoid comparison."

"Benjamin, I think my subconscious got the better of me."

"That's exactly what I was thinking, you old scoundrel!"

3

Château Blanzac was low and squat. No pointed towers, no mullioned windows, much less tall chimneys. The building's elegance lay in its symmetry and simplicity, along with the lovely tiling that ran beneath the vertigris roof.

A pair of two-hundred-year-old oak trees and three tall cedars dominated the grounds. Their branches caressed the sleepy country manor and its lichen-covered stones. Calling it a "château" was clearly deceptive. As for the titles of nobility claimed by its proprietor, there was no trace, aside from a wrought-iron coat of arms on the front-step railings, whose rust offset any hint of pretention. In the way of assets, the Castayracs owned only this home, with its few acres of vines and one-story outbuilding, along with the family title, which the baron liked to flaunt at the Biarritz casino on special occasions.

Benjamin pushed the doorbell. Its shrill ring set loose three large dogs, whose muzzles appeared at the windows. Benjamin scanned the surroundings. The vines hadn't been pruned. An antique Citroën DS 19 Pallas was parked in a garage, and on the right, a short distance from the outbuilding, four immense blackened walls stood silent. Burned beams, barrel hoops, and staves littered the frozen ground. Shards of glass, vestiges of the demijohns that had been turned into large Molotov cocktails, were everywhere. Benjamin could almost make out wisps of smoke amid the ruins. It had been less than two weeks since the catastrophe. Could the fire still be smoldering under this rubble? Its acrid vapors were stinging his throat.

The door remained hopelessly closed. Benjamin rang the bell again, more insistently this time. An imposing figure, despite the cane, finally appeared. Jean-Charles de Castayrac fit the image of a country squire that Benjamin had formed on his way from breakfast at the Bouglons. Minor provincial nobility, apparently bankrupt but intent on maintaining his status, even if it meant deluding people with window dressing, such as an old but shiny car, a tweed jacket missing a few buttons, a green felt hat, and a fine shirt frayed just a bit at the collar. Baron Castayrac stepped toward his visitors, shooing away the three Labradors.

"Don't worry, gentlemen. They don't bite. Athos, Porthos, Aramis: get lost! Go lie down! Down, I say!" The dogs ignored him and bounded out the door to greet the visitors. "Whom do I have the pleasure of speaking to?"

Benjamin introduced himself and his assistant. Right away, the baron's tone and expression became more gracious. A smile crossed his face.

"Please come in," he said. The cold was already turning his cheeks and hairy earlobes pink. "These dogs don't have enough sense to stay inside."

"No, it seems that they don't," Benjamin said, petting Porthos's black rump.

Virgile attempted to give the two other dogs a friendly pat, but they scooted past him and ran toward a building where a young man in a fur hat was watching from behind a Massey Ferguson tractor. He looked like a Russian peasant.

Without warning, the timid January sun seemed to dissipate entirely in the freezing weather. A thick cloud of condensation escaped from the baron's thin lips as he pointed his cane at the ruined wine cellar and lamented, "The work of a lifetime up in smoke. A damn shame."

Was it the cold or a surge of emotion that brought the tears to his eyes? Once in the shelter of the entryway, the baron removed his broad-rimmed hat and hung it on a hook next to a long dark coat. He did the same with his cane. He invited Benjamin and Virgile into his library without offering to take their coats. Two dueling embers were struggling in a tiny fireplace. Benjamin noticed that the bronze clock hopelessly showed twelve-thirty. Its pendulum was motionless. Had the baron deliberately left it unrepaired in the hope of banishing all notion of time from his home?

"Can I offer you anything?"

Benjamin picked up a begrudging tone in his voice. He sounded like a stingy host who had no more than a drop of port or cherry to share. There was no mention of Armagnac. Benjamin declined. Their meeting today was a formality, an initial contact. They would begin their review tomorrow, and Benjamin wanted to give Jean-Charles de Castayrac a heads-up. No doubt, he was still reeling from the nasty business of the fire and the loss of his salt-of-the-earth cellar master, Francisco.

"What a sad end, Mr. Cooker. Can you imagine? Perishing under such circumstances. It's all my fault."

"You have no reason to blame yourself, Mr. Castayrac," Benjamin said.

"And to think that I asked him to distill on Christmas Eve." The proprietor of Blanzac angrily grabbed the fireplace tongs to poke the few embers dying in the ashes.

Benjamin couldn't help thinking of his dear friend Eve, a television producer and classical music expert who had bought a magnificent château in Gers. The château had once belonged to the marquise of Montespan, and it had only one flaw. It was impossible to heat on the coldest days of winter.

"My dear Benjamin, all the forests of Gascony would not have enough lumber to keep my home warm with those high French ceilings," she joked. Benjamin had affectionately nicknamed her the Marquise de Shivering. That gave them both a good laugh, but at the time, it was summer, and they were sitting on the pleasantly warm terrace of Château de Beaumont.

It was just as bad in the baron's chilly library, which Benjamin figured was bearable only in the warmest months of the year. The *toile de jouy* wallpaper, with its repeated pastoral scene on a beige background, was slipping off the moldy plaster walls. The books and encyclopedias lining the shelves offered their musty edges to the no-tarial décor. Benjamin, who took pride in being something of a bibliophile, cast a wry look at an original edition of *Dictionary of Daily Life in the City and the Countryside*. Virgile had turned up the collar of his leather jacket.

"It's freezing in here," he whispered in his boss's ear.

If Jean-Charles de Castayrac heard Virgile, he didn't let on. "Please excuse the mess, but Blanzac is sorely lacking in women," he said. "Since the death of my wife, Elise, I have no interest in anything."

"Not even in bridge?" Benjamin asked, pointing to a card table where the baron had evidently enjoyed winning a game.

"Very rarely," he sighed. Benjamin thought he detected a hint of evasiveness in the old man's answer.

"You've never thought of remarrying, Mr. Castayrac?" Virgile asked.

Benjamin couldn't believe how socially clumsy Virgile could be sometimes. He couldn't tell the difference between a business client and a friend.

The baron had sunk into a decrepit Voltaire armchair. After blowing his nose on a muslin handkerchief, he stared long and hard at the cheeky assistant.

"I don't think either of my boys would have forgiven me. But my private life is my own business, and no one has the right to make judgments about what I've done or should have done."

"Please be patient with my assistant, Mr. Castayrac. Virgile Lanssien has all the candor of youth. Tact and diplomacy are sometimes optional, as far as he's concerned, and on this occasion, he dispensed with both," Benjamin quipped.

"That's regrettable," the petty noble responded.

Before Benjamin could say anything else, the man stood up and excused himself. He left the room and came back a few moments later with a bundle of vine shoots, which he tossed into the fireplace. The flames had no effect on the room's temperature. The baron turned on a lamp. Its shade smelled moldy. A cup of tea would not have been unwelcome, but the baron was clearly refraining from any superfluous hospitality. Benjamin and Virgile would have to make do with the quickly waning sparks.

On a white marble pedestal table, the face of a plain woman was encased in a garnet-colored velour frame. Lady Castayrac looked smug in her three-strand pearl choker. Her large forehead and slightly flat nose bespoke peasant origins. Blanzac owed its prosperity to her. The Armagnac cellar, the central heating—when the boiler was still functioning—the Citroën DS 19, the tractor, and much more had all been purchased with her family's money. That very noon, Beatrice and Philippe de Bouglon had given Benjamin and Virgile a detailed account of how this family had enriched itself.

In the seventeenth century, the Riquets de Lauze had made a fortune in water. A gift from God had sprung up from their land. On the wild fields of the Quercy, a region north of Gascony covered with dense forests and dark rocks where goats and sheep roamed in the junipers, a diviner had come upon waters whose curative powers were said to be astonishing. After drinking just one cup, the diviner managed to completely detoxify his system and relieve his chronic constipation. This place, called Alvignac—more specifically Salmière—quickly became a destination for pilgrims from the nearby regions of Corrèze, Aveyron, and even Cantal, all of whom arrived with bottles and flasks to hold this body-cleansing nectar.

The family began offering their water with miraculous laxative powers the same way they did their aromatic truffles: for cold, hard cash. To promote the spring, they invited the exquisitely elegant Marquise de Pompadour, King Louis XV's chief mistress, to Alvignac. Immediately, Versailles and Paris were abuzz with talk of this water, which was fortified with calcium, sodium, and magnesium, according to the scientists from the Sorbonne.

Louis de Rouvroy, the duke of Saint-Simon, wrote in his memoirs that if there were one boring place on earth that he would gladly visit, it was Alvignac, because he could overeat and not get fat, thanks to the water. Three centuries later, the French writer Pierre Benoit wrote the same thing in his colorful *Lunch at Sousceyrac*. The reputation of the waters of Salmière never waned, and it continued to draw famous writers and even quite a few politicians. Like gas in a stomach, the Riquets' fortune swelled. They wouldn't have been able to stuff all the cash under their mattresses or into their wool stockings even if they had wanted to. It went into the bank and finally fell into the hands of Elise Riquet de Lauze.

As cupid's game of love would have it, she married a Castayrac, whose specialty was trading in eau-de-vie. The dowry was much more beautiful than the bride, and the groom was more talented in manners than business. The couple experienced a few years of happiness and had two sons, Alban and Valmont, three or four good vintages, and then a rash of disappointments, serious breaches in the marriage contract, and finally the agonies of illness. Breast cancer claimed the miraculous springs heiress. She died on a Good Friday at the age of forty-four without having embraced her two children one last time. The whole town of Labastide-d'Armagnac accompanied her hearse to the Castayrac family vault on a dismal spring day.

"Mr. Castayrac, how much eau-de-vie would you say you lost in the fire?" Benjamin ventured, barely looking at the baron.

"That is difficult to judge, sir. Only Francisco would have been able to tell you to the exact liter," Castayrac said, rubbing his fingers along the moth-eaten armrests. "He kept the books."

"Nevertheless, you're the one who takes care of the accounting, taxes, and the administrative details, aren't you?"

"Or maybe it's your sons?" suggested Virgile.

"Mr. Lanssien, I'd prefer to answer your superior. It's a matter of principle. In this house, only the elders have the right to speak."

"So it's Alban we'd need to—"

"That's enough, Virgile," Benjamin interrupted.

The baron smirked, apparently pleased to have established his authority.

"Francisco was—how can I put it—part of the family," the baron said, looking only at Benjamin. "My father, Jean-Sébastien de Castayrac, thought the boy had an honest face and hired him. Francisco wasn't even sixteen when he walked through the gate. He came from the foothills of the Pyrenees, from Jurançon, where he had been a farm boy. His parents had fled Franco's Spain."

Benjamin nodded. "Do you know anything else about his background?"

"Francisco Vasquez was a private man. He rarely confided in anyone. He had a saying: 'All I know, I put in a bottle!' Even now I can hear him speaking those words with his Aragonese accent."

"He became your cellar master, and no offense intended, I believe he crafted your best eau-de-vie."

"I am indebted to him for many things," Jean-Charles de Castayrac said and sighed. "And one of them is the quality of my Armagnacs."

"Did he live in the château?"

"A few months after he arrived in Blanzac, my father gave him a shack near the old stables that the day workers had used for their breaks during haymaking season and the grape harvest. He never paid any rent. That's how it was. Francisco was family. He often ate lunch with us. That is, when my wife was still alive, because after... After, we made other arrangements."

"He never married?" Benjamin asked, reading his silenced assistant's mind.

"No," the baron said. "But he was never short on girls. They all flocked around him. He was good-looking. Well, that's history now."

"I heard he sowed his seed all over Labastide," Benjamin said with a touch of mischief.

"That's what they say, all right. But people exaggerate. If you believe everything that's said in town... I'm sure some people are whispering that I started the fire in my own wine cellar to collect the insurance."

Virgile spoke up again. "And what were you doing on December 24th?"

The baron crossed his legs, revealing mismatched socks and hairy white calves. He stared at Benjamin without blinking.

Benjamin broke the silence. "As far as the insurance is concerned, the fire was an accident. I'm here to get things moving, Mr. Castayrac. I am counting on your cooperation."

"You'll have it, Mr. Cooker."

"I don't doubt it. I suggest that we meet tomorrow morning to draw up an initial assessment of the reserves that were burned."

"Don't come at the crack of dawn. I like to stay under the covers when it's this cold outside."

"I understand. How about ten o'clock? Will that do?"

"I'd prefer eleven," the baron responded. He then sprang nimbly from his chair and headed toward the vestibule.

The winemaker wondered what use the cane could possibly served, other than that of pompous accessory. Evidently, the proprietor of Blanzac was a better actor than vintner. Was it possible that the fire was not an accident?

The parting was cool and barely polite.

4

Benjamin needed no persuasion to accept Philippe de Bouglon's offer to stay a few nights at Prada, just enough time to assess the loss sustained by the Castayrac estate. With his friend's Gascon gift of gab, the quality of their Armagnacs, Beatrice's undeniable culinary talents, and the magnificence of his old friend's humidor, how could he resist? Naturally, Benjamin didn't intend to hurry his assessment. He'd take his time to dig just a little deeper. But there was still the matter of Virgile.

"Young man, you are welcome to stay in the tower. We have a small room there," Philippe said.

"Honey, that won't work, the pipes have frozen. He wouldn't have any water," Beatrice said.

"Besides, isn't that bedroom the one that's haunted?" Benjamin added with a wink.

"I'm fine staying somewhere in town, boss."

"There's a family in Labastide-d'Armagnac, the Cantarels, who have guest rooms," Philippe said. "You'll be happy as a clam there. The rooms are very simple but comfortable. The owner is friendly and, to be honest, a bit chatty. She has a son about your age. He's the striker for the Cazaubon team, a champion rugby player. He was named the best player in Gascony. But Virgile, maybe you're not a fan?"

"As a matter of fact, I played two seasons for the Bergerac club."

"What position?" Philippe asked.

"Wing," Virgile responded, thrusting out his chest a bit.

Benjamin was amused. "Philippe, how far away is it?"

"Less than five minutes from here."

With a wink, Beatrice assured Virgile that he could have his meals at Prada. She was already talking to him as though he were a dear member of the clan.

"And Evelyne Cantarel will tell you more about Blanzac," she said. "She worked for the Castayracs for many years. Evelyne's a nice woman who hasn't had an easy life. She and her son live with her father, who's still hale and hearty. I think he's even the local agent for the Protection Insurance, isn't he, Philippe?"

Benjamin smiled politely and fiddled with his glass. Why hadn't the insurance company mentioned the local agent?

"I'm not sure, Beatrice. I think he quit a short time ago," Philippe said. "Benjamin, most of us around here are covered by the Social Agricultural

Insurance. At any rate, when it comes to insurance, we are always at their mercy."

Beatrice called Evelyne Cantarel to make Virgile's lodging arrangements. Evelyne was delighted to have a new guest, especially in low season. No, he did not drink tea in the morning. He drank coffee. How long would he be staying? Hard to say. Three days, maybe four or five...

Before Virgile departed, Benjamin and he had dinner with the Bouglons. On the menu: shirred eggs and cheese from the Pyrenees, which went especially well with the Baron de Bachen white they served, a good representative of wines from Tursan.

"Virgile, my boy, what do you know about this wine?" Benjamin asked.

"Hmm," Virgile said, swirling the straw-colored liquid in his glass and bringing it to his nose. "Fruit... Mango, I'd say, with some citrus notes, floral aromas, and a slight hint of honey." He sipped and swished before adding, "Round, but refreshing. I'd say baroque grapes, sauvignon, and... I'm not sure, another variety, but what?"

"Very good," Philippe interjected. "Petit and gros manseng."

Benjamin nodded. "The property in the Landes region dates back to the thirteenth century," he said. "In 1983, the famous restaurateur Michel Guérard bought the estate. He replanted the vineyards in 1985, for a first harvest in 1988. He's helped to revive the appellation."

"Benjamin, I'm quite impressed by Virgile," Philippe said. "He must be quite an asset."

"I'm not so sure you'd say that if you knew the extent of his ignorance when it comes to Armagnac," Benjamin said.

"Boss! What about 'All for one and one for all'? You're supposed to be on my side, especially now that we're in Gascony, the land of *The Three Musketeers*."

"My boy, you may also remember this from the same book: 'Never fear quarrels, but seek adventure.' I believe we have an adventure set for us tomorrow. Isn't that right, Philippe?"

"Yes, the mobile distiller is coming at the crack of dawn."

Virgile glanced from Philippe at Benjamin and then at Beatrice. "The mobile distiller?"

"That's right. In Armagnac, many distillers don't actually have their own stills. Roving distillers take their alembic from farm to farm and distill according to each cellar master's specifications. Here we always distill in early January," Beatrice explained.

The simple feast wound down, and Benjamin, Virgile, and the Bouglons called it a night shortly after dinner.

Benjamin handed over his keys to the Mercedes convertible, and Philippe gave the directions to the guest house. "When you leave Prada, just go to Place Royale, and take the Rue du Café-Chantant.

The first right is the Rue des Taillandiers. Take it. The Cantarels live in a half-timber house. You can't miss it."

Benjamin retired to his room, where he called Elisabeth to tell her that he would probably be staying longer than he had expected.

§ § §

The sound of a tractor maneuvering in the courtyard woke Benjamin, who had never been a heavy sleeper. He peered out the window at a dawn sky that was purple and rooftops that were painted with frost. Benjamin's room was frigid, and even though he was wide awake, he wasn't looking forward to the prospect of crawling out from under the covers. Fortunately, the aroma of coffee was beginning to creep under the door, and his excitement over the event unfolding outside soon overpowered his desire for comfort. His shower could wait. He wouldn't miss this for anything.

Philippe, gesturing dramatically and yelling "whoa," was guiding the still into the wine cellar. It was a strange-looking contraption, all copper and bedecked with pipes, coils, and odd gauges.

When Benjamin joined them, Philippe introduced the distiller, a cross-eyed bearded man named René Dardolive. He would be the master of ceremonies. Benjamin couldn't guess his age, but he looked prematurely bald, something he was trying to hide under a shapeless black felt hat. René was speechless when Philippe announced the celebrated winemaker's presence.

In the half-light of the wine cellar, Beatrice and Philippe bustled about, carrying blocks of oak for the boiler. Soon, esoteric permutations would be under way, supervised by the alchemist in a khaki hunting jacket. René had learned his craft from his father. The Dardolive men had been distillers for many generations, and *aygue vive*, or living water, was no mystery to this quiet man. He had been weaned on the vapors of a zealously polished still.

Dardolive was set to begin his rite of offering the wine from the Bouglons' harvest to distillation. But first Beatrice called everyone to the table: ham, duck cracklings, rabbit and boar pâté, scrambled eggs, red wine, and hot coffee. Virgile showed up, looking groggy at this unlikely hour, when night hadn't yet buried its last demons. Evelyne Cantarel had prepared a copious breakfast for him, but Benjamin knew his assistant wouldn't be able to resist Beatrice's terrines.

Benjamin could see the anticipation in Virgile's eyes. Distillation was something Virgile had studied but never seen. Now he was about to witness this miracle for himself. A pure and crystalline eau-de-vie would soon be flowing through the murmuring copper still.

Despite his rough manners and silences, René managed to exchange a few words with Virgile.

"Did you ever distill for the Château Blanzac?" Virgile asked.

René took a gulp of coffee and wiped his mouth on his sleeve. "Nope. They got their own still. Francisco did good work."

"Yes, what a terrible accident."

"It ain't no accident, I'm telling you. That family's as twisted as an alembic."

Without any further explanation, René rose from the table to get to work. He filled the boiler with water, just enough to start the process. Then he connected the loader vat to a pot topped with a still-head fitted with a long swan's-neck pipe. He lit the fire, feeding it vine shoots first and then old stumps. When the blaze was finally roaring, he threw in large pieces of dry oak. The distillation could begin. Philippe leaned toward Virgile and began a running commentary.

"This is a continuous still. It's made of pure copper and distills only once," he said.

"Cognac gets distilled twice, that I know," Virgile said. "Is it copper because of its superior heat conduction?"

"That's right. This continuous distillation is actually quite simple," Philippe continued. "René here feeds the wine from the loader vat into the still, where it goes through the bottom of the cooling apparatus. It fills the preheater, then descends through the heating column, flowing over a number of plates and ending up in the boiler. This is when René removes the wine residue. The intense heat causes the wine to boil, and the vapor rises up through the incoming wine to the top of the still. In the process it becomes richer in alcohol and picks up the wine's aromatic substances. Then it flows through the condensing coils, where it's cooled. The resulting eau-de-vie is deliciously fruit-scented, with some floral notes. It's fiery with youth and needs some time to develop its complexity and mildness. A bit like us, in the end."

Philippe's cheeks were flushed from the heat. Standing back a bit, Benjamin was listening to the lesson. Just when he was about to say something, Philippe started talking again.

"Once the alcohol level is stabilized, the still can function continuously. It can change wine into Armagnac day and night without stopping."

"So the distiller's work is pretty much done?" Virgile asked.

Benjamin could see that his assistant was feigning naiveté to encourage his host to continue talking. Virgile knew more than he was letting on.

"Not at all," Philippe responded. "This is precisely where his craftsmanship comes in. He understands everything about the vapors and the heat exchange happening in the coils. He sees nothing but knows everything."

Philippe continued in a hushed tone. "He's a magician, I tell you. Now and then he consults the alcoholmeter, which allows him to verify the alcohol content, but for the most part he uses his intuition and his senses. He listens. He feels the heater to gauge the heat. He uses his nose, too, and he tastes the product from time to time. He is constantly on the alert."

Benjamin took over. "His main concern is keeping the flow of wine just right. Despite all the heat, distillation is a gentle process. It must not be disturbed."

For an hour, the still murmured and bubbled. Those watching fell silent from time to time. Finally, Philippe led Virgile to a copper faucet, which was emitting a thin, aromatic steam of eau-de-vie.

"Smell this, young man!"

Virgile sniffed it. "I pick up plum jam and white flowers," he said.

"Those aromas, plus fragrances of grape and pear, are characteristic of the folle-blanche grape," Philippe said, with pride evident in his blue-gray eyes.

"What is the alcohol content?" Benjamin asked.

"Fifty-five percent," Philippe responded.

René Dardolive had removed his hunting jacket and was working in his shirtsleeves. He looked like an organist adjusting the pedals and bellows of his instrument. His movements were precise and impressive as he tended the still, controlling all aspects of the gurgling, hissing, and murmuring machine.

Philippe told Benjamin that it had been a good year for Prada, and René would need at least two days to get through the estate's seven casks, each with four hundred liters of wine. The winemaker and his friend decided to step outside for a few minutes to catch a breath of fresh air, leaving Virgile behind, captivated by the scene.

§ § §

Virgile turned to say something to Benjamin and realized that his boss was nowhere to be found. He left the wine cellar to search for him, heading first to the Prada kitchen, where Beatrice was busy preparing the noon meal. He had no idea what was simmering over low heat in the Dutch oven, but the aroma was tantalizing.

"I think they're in Philippe's office. They're setting the world right. But first, run to the Cantarels. Evelyne called. You need your key to the house in case nobody's around to let you in."

Virgile opened the kitchen door. "Shit. It's cold!" Virgile cursed, pulling his wool hat over his ears and buttoning up his sheepskin coat. He'd heard the news on Beatrice's kitchen radio. It confirmed what he had already suspected. The thermometer had dipped to a bone-chilling minus ten degrees the previous night, and school busing had been suspended. He rushed to the car and drove through the village, which seemed deserted. Everyone in their right mind was inside.

When Virgile arrived at Evelyne Cantarel's house, he found her in a floral apron, polishing the cherrywood buffet in the dining room with beeswax.

"When you don't have a head, you have to have..."

"Legs, I know," Virgile replied with a smile.

The woman put down her rag, which smelled slightly of rancid honey, and offered her guest a cup of coffee.

"I don't know if I have time."

"Why would you want to rush back outside in this cold?" the Gascon woman asked.

Virgile decided to tell her why he was in Labastide: the business at Blanzac, the damage suffered, the visit to the château... Evelyne Cantarel pulled a porcelain cup from the buffet and poured Virgile some coffee. She waved to a chair, wordlessly telling him to have a seat. Continuing to sip her own coffee from an old mustard jar, she plopped down in a nearby chair.

"Tell me, how is it at the château, Mr. Virgile?"

"What do you mean? The atmosphere?"

"No, the housekeeping."

"Well, it's a bit neglected. The place doesn't appear to be dusted regularly." Virgile didn't know what else to say. He had never given housekeeping much attention.

"When the missus was alive, everything was impeccable. We had to polish the copper every week, and we waxed the floors on the fifteenth of every month."

"It's changed a lot, then," Virgile replied, giving the woman who had once taken care of Château Blanzac a nod meant to show his respect for her work.

"And the baron? Still just as..."

Virgile saw no harm in confiding more. A second cup of coffee might even take the chill off. His boss could wait.

"Spry? Yes, he doesn't seem as old as his years."

"Oh, widowhood is not his problem! When La Riquette died, he got over it pretty quickly."

"La Riquette?"

"Yes, Mrs. Riquet...de Lauze. Forgive the nickname. At the Castayracs, we called them La Riquette and the Robber Baron, if you understand what I mean."

"I see," Virgile said, all smiles.

"But you're going to think I'm a gossip."

"It's only gossip if it's speculation and rumor. As far as I'm concerned, you're giving me the facts."

"That's what my father thinks. Maybe you'll meet him tonight. He spends most of his time hunting these days."

"Wood pigeons?"

"No, woodcocks. They're more challenging, but he's still limber for his age."

Evelyne got up to make another pot of coffee and stoke the wood-burning stove, whose flames were dying down.

"Did you see the sons?"

"One of them, I think. A young man, kind of shy with pale eyes. He didn't come to meet us."

"That had to be Valmont. He still lives there."

"What's the other one like?"

"Alban? He's a Castayrac through and through. A bit standoffish, a loudmouth, ambitious, thinks he's hot stuff. He's really his father's son. He married well to the only daughter of the Nadaillac family. They claim they're descendants of D'Artagnan, the fourth musketeer. It's been five years now, and there's still no bun in the oven. Folks say the bride won't have anything to do with her husband."

"Maybe they just need a little time. Children don't always happen right away." Virgile felt a little self-conscious saying this. What did he know about marriage?

"I doubt that it has anything to do with timing, Mr. Virgile. The Castayracs behave in bed the same way they do at a banquet. As soon as they're served, they're looking at their neighbor's plate, if you know what I mean. That would be enough to make any bride turn her back to her husband at night."

"I know exactly what you mean," Virgile said, discreetly glancing at his watch. His coffee was getting cold, and he was losing interest in the conversation.

"I've taken up too much of your time with all my stories," Evelyne said. Still, it was clear that she wanted him to stay. She took another tack, changing the conversation to the baron's business. "Do you think, after all that's happened, that he'll end up being chairman?"

"Chairman of what?"

"Chairman of the committee, of course!"

"You mean the Armagnac Promotion Committee?"

"He's been wanting that plum for so long. Imagine—the baron heading an organization that has such an influential say in producing and regulating all our eau-de-vie. And to think that his main rival is Aymeric de Nadaillac, his own son's father-in-law."

"Correct me if I'm wrong, but you don't seem to be very fond of the Castayracs."

"It's ancient history, Mr. Virgile. The day isn't long enough to tell you all that I know."

The woman in the floral apron rose from her chair. Virgile thought her eyes looked misty. Not wanting to embarrass her by staring, he looked away. On a side table, he spotted a badly framed photograph: two rows of proud-looking and powerfully built young men.

"That's the Cazaubon rugby team, and that one there, on the left, is my son, my little Joachim!"

"Little! He looks quite athletic to me. I used to play too."

"Really, what team?"

"Bergerac."

"So you and Joachim have something in common. I can't wait for you to meet him. Joachim just loves the sport and his teammates." Evelyne's eyes were shining with pride. "They threw him a big birthday party last August."

"You don't say. My birthday's in August too."

"No kidding. What day?"

"August 31."

"I can't believe it. Joachim's birthday is August 31. This is unbelievable. The same sport, the same birthday..."

"Yes, it is quite a coincidence, isn't it? You could call us brothers in spirit." Virgile hoped she wouldn't try to find something else that he shared with her son. He really needed to leave. He stood, thanked her for the coffee, grabbed his coat, and headed to the door.

"You forgot your key again, Mr. Virgile!"

Virgile slapped his cheek. "I'm such a nitwit. You'd think I'd remember this time. Thank you."

Evelyne Cantarel took his arm and pulled him toward her. "Your being here is a sign from heaven," she said. "May I give you a hug?"

5

At Château Blanzac, the baron's welcome was even cooler than it was the day before. Castayrac was dressed for business in a well-cut three-piece suit made from fine dark wool, and although Benjamin told him that Virgile and he needed to interview him at length and go through the rubble of the destroyed wine cellar, the baron made it clear that he had more important things to do.

Jean-Charles de Castayrac intended to reduce this meeting to a simple formality. The man was pressed for time, and he left no doubt that his attire was not for the benefit of his honored guest, even if Benjamin was the most famous winemaker in France. The board of directors of the Armagnac Promotion Committee was convening at Eauze that very afternoon, and the election of its new chairman was on the agenda. The matter would be decided during a lunch preceding the meeting at a fine restaurant named Pépita's. Benjamin Cooker would not make him late.

Benjamin sent Virgile to the wine cellar and proceeded with his questions. "How many casks, Mr. Castayrac, would you estimate that you lost?"

Castayrac paced the room, hands behind his back, chafing at each of Benjamin's inquiries regarding his exact losses. "I already told you, Mr. Cooker. We lost thirty-six."

"Are you quite sure?"

"Absolutely. And I lost all those demijohns, most of which I inherited from my ancestors. They were famous eau-de-vies, highly prized by collectors. Their alcohol content was between forty and fifty percent. Some dated back to 1869. Napoleon III loved them. Do you realize how valuable they were?"

"A real treasure," the winemaker agreed.

"You can say that again, Mr. Cooker!"

"How many of those demijohns did you have in your reserves?"

"I could not say precisely, but more than sixty at the very least."

"Had they all been duly declared?"

"Francisco took care of those details."

"That's putting a lot of trust in him," Benjamin said. He wrote some numbers in his spiral notebook.

"As I said, Mr. Vasquez was considered a member of the family. I never doubted his word."

"Yes, but unfortunately the only thing we have to go on is your word, since your books were destroyed. Moreover, I've been doing this work for quite a while, and this is the first time I've heard of a vineyard owner leaving all his records in his wine cellar."

"How could I have known that my wine cellar—and my office, along with it—would go up in smoke? What are you insinuating, Mr. Cooker?"

"I'm not insinuating anything. I'm just trying to gather information and understand what happened. Failing your cooperation, I shall be forced to proceed with the investigation as I see fit."

Benjamin put down his notebook and scanned the library shelves. Castayrac struck him as a man who liked to collect books and show them off but didn't read very much. He felt the baron's eyes on him. The man was standing in front of the fireplace, which was filled with gray ashes. He hadn't even bothered to light a fire for the winemaker and his assistant.

"If we take a safe and pragmatic approach, sir, we can say that you lost 14,400 liters of Armagnac in casks and six hundred in ten-liter demijohns. In all, then, that gives us fifteen thousand liters, a good round number."

"That must be pretty close," the baron said brusquely.

The Labradors were barking in the courtyard. But there was nothing but silence in the dark and bitterly cold library, where the two men were challenging each other without making eye contact. Finally, Benjamin said, "At this stage of the assessment, we need to allow for evaporation, the amount taken by the angels." He raised his eyes.

"Of course," Castayrac responded, a half-smile on his dry lips.

"I will have to apply the formula devised by the Directorate-General of Customs and Indirect Taxes: six percent per year."

"Do you want to ruin me?" the baron said, raising his voice.

"If you had been able to give me a precise accounting of the different reserves and which vintages they came from, we might have come up with a better estimate. But as it stands, Mr. Castayrac, it's a guessing game, and we'll have to agree on a figure based more or less on what we believe you lost in this terrible fire."

"Good God!" Castayrac responded.

Before he could say anything else, a man with a thin face, short hair, and steel-blue eyes walked into the library, a cigarillo between his fingers. The baron frowned, but went ahead with an introduction. "Allow me, Mr. Cooker, to introduce my older son, Alban."

"It's a pleasure," the baron's son said, extending his hand.

Castayrac hadn't bothered to shake his hand the day before, when he arrived at Blanzac. Benjamin wondered if this warmer greeting meant that the son didn't resent his presence as much as the father. But then again, maybe it only meant that his mother had taught him his manners.

"Father, you'll come down with pneumonia sooner or later if you don't start heating this château."

"Must I remind you, Alban, that the boiler is broken, and I don't have the finances to get a new one?"

"That doesn't mean you can't make a fire in the fireplace." Alban started filling the firebox with old vine stocks.

"That's enough! I've seen enough flames lately."

"As you wish, but you can't allow yourself to get sick if you ever want to lead that committee."

Alban de Castayrac turned to Benjamin. "I believe my father-in-law is going to run, too, and he has a good chance of winning."

"Get out!" the baron shouted.

The older Castayrac son gave Benjamin a sly look before leaving the room. "So long, Mr. Cooker. I'm sure we'll meet again."

The winemaker had hardly expected such animosity between the father and his son. He didn't have much sympathy for either of them. Caught forever in the framed photograph on the pedestal table, Castayrac's deceased wife, wearing her self-righteous expression, seemed to be chastising her husband.

The widower had enshrouded himself in an obstinate silence. Benjamin cleared his throat, played with the cap of his pen, and finally picked up his notebook to scribble some words, which he underlined twice.

Then the taciturn baron peered at his watch.

"I'm already late for my lunch," he said, suggesting that Benjamin return later in the afternoon.

"At cocktail hour," he said unctuously.

Summarily dismissed, Benjamin pulled up the collar of his Loden. Cocktail hour at this château would no doubt be as cold as the baron's library. He headed for the burned-out wine cellar, where Virgile was still looking for clues in the ashes. His clothes were smudged from searching through the oak staves that the fire had not completely incinerated.

"I counted exactly nineteen demijohns, boss. I found the necks and have something to show for it." With a grimace, he opened his right hand. A bloody gash ran along his palm.

"Holy smoke, you have to disinfect that right away. Are you vaccinated against tetanus?"

"Yes, I think so."

"You think so, or you're sure?" Benjamin asked.

A figure stepped out from behind the garage housing the old DS. Benjamin recognized the young man from the day before. He had a flask of Armagnac in one hand, and in the other he had a white handkerchief. He went to Virgile and without waiting for consent doused the wound with eau-de-vie. Virgile let out a howl. His caregiver smiled as he held him firmly by the wrist.

"Don't be a sissy, Virgile," Benjamin said. He turned to the country medic. "You're Valmont, aren't you?"

The young man nodded while pouring more antiseptic on the wound. He carefully folded the handkerchief to make a compress and applied it to Virgile's hand. Virgile grimaced again. His eyes were brimming with tears.

"It's nothing. Don't make such a fuss!" Valmont de Castayrac ordered in a coarse tone.

His features were rough, his eyes pale, and his lips thick. The second son of the estate completely ignored Benjamin's questions and answered only Virgile's. Even then he was noncommittal. "I don't know anything," he said. "The day of the fire, I was hunting for woodcock in the Fatsillières Forest. When I got back, the cellar was blazing."

"You were hunting on Christmas Eve?" Virgile asked.

"Yes, people around here think nothing of hunting the day before Christmas. If we bag something, it winds up on the table the next day. Now let me go look for some gauze and adhesive tape. I'll be right back."

Valmont hurried toward the house. Benjamin, meanwhile, figured this was an opportunity to get a closer look at the DS. He was a car collector at heart and had quickly identified the model: a 1957 Citroën DS-19 with a gearshift on the steering wheel. The four-cylinder engine had stood the test of time with its inimitable aerodynamics. Benjamin would have gladly offered to buy it from the baron, who could have used the money. He tried to recall the name of the Italian who had designed the body of this astonishingly futuristic jewel, but his memory failed him.

When Benjamin returned from the garage, Virgile's hand was bandaged. He was absorbed in counting the iron hoops from the fire-ravaged casks. Valmont was at his side, helping him with the metal scraps and heaps of wood.

"Tell me, Valmont, is the DS in the garage one of the first models?" Benjamin asked, trying to sound naïve.

"Exactly! A 1957. It's a collector's piece. The most beautiful car Flaminio Bertoni ever designed."

"I see you are a connoisseur," the winemaker said.

"Well, let's say it's a hobby."

At that moment, Benjamin Cooker realized that he would never own the Castayracs' navy-blue DS. "Drop it, Dad!" his daughter Margaux would have told him. "Not even in your dreams!"

Oddly, the disappointment whetted his appetite. He asked Virgile to take a break and join him for a Gascon lunch at Pépita's, whose foie gras ravioli was said to be excellent.

"Your 280 SL isn't bad, either," said Valmont, who had walked out with them to Benjamin's Mercedes.

Surprised by the remark, the winemaker was quick to respond. "I assure you, young man, it's not for sale!"

Valmont de Castayrac was just as quick to reply. "And neither is the DS-19." Having already given Virgile his handkerchief, Valmont pulled a wadded tissue from his pocket and wiped his dripping nose.

Put in his place and feeling glum, Benjamin felt for his keys and handed them to his assistant, who declined the offer.

"If it's okay with you, boss, with my hand and all, I'd prefer that you take the wheel."

"Oh, of course, Virgile."

As they passed through the estate's rusty gate, Benjamin glimpsed the silhouette in the rearview mirror of the true and only caretaker of Château Blanzac. The younger and crafty Castayrac could read minds. It would be wise to be careful around him.

6

"I am very sorry, but we're full," the restaurant owner said, looking exhausted but acting gracious nevertheless.

The dining room was filled with boisterous voices and the clatter of knives and forks. The conversation at the long table dominating the room was free-flowing. The faces of the diners were flushed from all the alcohol, and they had unbuttoned their shirt collars—the better to enjoy this midday feast. Busy servers filled their glasses as quickly as the men emptied them.

Benjamin Cooker instantly recognized Jean-Charles de Castayrac, who ignored him. At the head of the table, a distinguished-looking man with a white mane and aquiline nose appeared to be orchestrating the proceedings. He had a medal of honor pin in his lapel. Probably the agricultural merit award, Benjamin surmised. With his salt-and-pepper goatee, he resembled a musketeer, a highly regarded figure in these parts. Benjamin guessed that he was Aymeric de Nadaillac, father-in-law of Alban de Castayrac.

The description Philippe would give him that same night would confirm his hunch.

"Try your luck at Au Trou Gascon. It's a mile from here," the woman suggested. By the looks of her apron, Benjamin imagined that she officiated in the kitchen, as well as the dining room.

Leaving the inn, Virgile teased Benjamin. "I guess we won't be enjoying any foie gras ravioli today."

"Maybe that's not such a bad thing," Benjamin muttered. "We are here to work, after all."

"We won't be getting the inside scoop on the Armagnac committee either. You know, boss, my mom taught me not to eavesdrop."

Benjamin didn't deign to respond. Virgile turned away and started peeling off the bandage Valmont had wrapped around his hand. Patience had never been one of Virgile's virtues.

"Just let it alone for now, Virgile," Benjamin said. "We haven't finished our work at the château, and I don't want you getting that hand infected."

Fortunately, Au Trou Gascon more than satisfied their appetites. The waitress was plump and eager to please. "How is it?" she asked time and again. "Do you need anything else?" This finally exasperated the winemaker, who just wanted to enjoy his meal.

Virgile grinned, hardly looking up from his guinea fowl with wild mushrooms. After a few minutes of silence, he gave Benjamin his assessment of the Castayrac cellar. In his eyes, the only tangible elements were the barrel hoops. With four to a cask, it was easy to estimate the number the baron's paradise had housed, assuming they were all full. As for the demijohns, he had managed to locate nineteen bottle necks. At best, twenty demijohns, swaddled in their wicker casings, had been tucked away in storage.

The assistant took a paper napkin and scribbled a series of numbers. When he was done, Benjamin put on his reading glasses to take a look. Satisfied with the final figures, he copied the calculations into his notebook.

"Good work, Virgile. It seems that we're far from the figures Castayrac gave us. His numbers are significantly higher—three times higher as far as the demijohns are concerned. It's a classic ploy: pad the reserves to bring the business back to an even keel and enjoy the serendipitous flow of cash from the insurance company. And then he can plead ignorance under the pretext that Francisco was the one in charge of the books."

"Yes, but to take us for idiots! I don't care if he's a baron. I'm going to let him know that we're onto his game."

"You're not going to say anything, Virgile."

"Why shouldn't I?"

"It's better not to rush things. We still need to gather evidence."

"But, boss, we have the proof."

"Of insurance fraud, perhaps. But I want to know more. Just to make sure we're not missing something."

Benjamin fell quiet. He had opted for coffee and was now staring at the bottom of his cup. The winemaker's habit of silently musing sometimes irritated his assistant, who always wanted to know what he was thinking. But Benjamin continued to peer into his cup, as if the solution to his investigation lay there.

"I must tell you, I'm not very good at reading coffee grounds," Virgile said.

"I suggest a few drops of Armagnac in the bottom of our cups, Virgile. Perhaps a fresh idea will wind up staring us in the face."

The winemaker called the waitress and ordered a Laberdolive. Benjamin had only to request the vintage from Virgile's year of birth to make his protégé's face light up. Benjamin poured a few drops of the very amber Armagnac into each coffee cup, ignoring the two balloon glasses brought by the young woman.

"I have a hunch," Virgile murmured, "that some liquor might just loosen the baron's tongue."

"I think the same thing, Virgile. But for now, tell me what this eau-de-vie brings to your nose."

"Quince, definitely," Virgile said.

"Exactly!" Benjamin responded. "I will add: quince paste, and little by little, it tends toward prune, doesn't it?"

"I'm staying with quince. Perhaps with a hint of lime?"

"Do you know, Virgile, how the Latin poet who shares your name described the quince?"

"No idea."

"He described it as 'pale with tender down.' Lovely, isn't it? He was referring to the fuzzy skin, of course."

"Since we're displaying our knowledge, do you know where people used to plant quince trees?" Virgile asked, mischief written on his lips.

Benjamin shook his head, feeling a bit embarrassed because he didn't know the answer.

Virgile was quick to fill him in. "Quince trees were often planted in the corners of a vegetable garden to officially mark where the plot ended."

Benjamin smiled at the play on words in French, the word for quince, *coign*, sounding the same as the one for corner, *coin*.

Finishing his Armagnac, Benjamin glanced out the window. The sky looked as ashen as the rubble in the Blanzac cellar. Farmers in the area were predicting that a change in temperature would accompany the new moon. On this point, their waitress happily concurred.

"The weather's going to get milder," she said as Benjamin paid the bill and buttoned up his Loden.

It had become obvious that this gracious and well-endowed waitress was none other than the owner. The food and the Armagnac had restored the winemaker's spirits, and he was sure that he would be seeing this woman and her restaurant again. The marinated duck had been a real treat, the duck breast cooked to perfection.

"So, Virgile, how was that?" Benjamin asked, grinning as Virgile and he slipped into the beige leather seats of the Mercedes. Benjamin started the car and turned on the radio. The local news was on.

> In a surprise upset this afternoon, Aymeric de Nadaillac was elected chairman of the Armagnac Promotion Committee by an overwhelming major-ity of those voting. Albert Pesquidoux, outgoing president of the APC, had backed his rival, Jean-Charles de Castayrac, owner of Château Blanzac. Nadaillac is the father-in-law of Alban de Castayrac, the baron's elder son. Château Blanzac's cellars were burned to the ground in December, and cellar master Francisco Vasquez died in that fire. An investigation conducted by the Saint-Justin Police Department concluded that an explosion in the still caused the fire.

"The baron may not be in the mood to see us," Benjamin said.

"I won't argue with that. Boss, can you drop me off at the Cantarels? I need a shower after spending the morning in all that rubble. And frankly, I don't think I'm needed at your meeting with the losing candidate for chairman of the Armagnac Promotion Committee. Unless you object, of course."

Without saying a word, Benjamin turned left at the first fork in the road and headed toward Labastide-d'Armagnac. He let his assistant out at the front entry to the half-timber house. He imagined a cozy room fragrant with a wood fire and goose fat. In his mind, he saw copper pans shining on a wall and a hanging lamp casting a golden circle of light on the table. A figure at one of the windows caught the winemaker's eye. It had to be Evelyne Cantarel. No doubt, she was pleased to see the return of her houseguest.

§ § §

"What happened to you, Mr. Virgile?" Evelyne Cantarel cried when she saw the young man's bandaged hand.

"It's nothing, Mrs. Cantarel, just a little work accident. Nothing serious."

"Let me have a look."

Just as she was peeling away the bandage, a man came into the room. He was wearing brown corduroy pants and a heavy jacquard sweater.

Under his hoary eyebrows were two mouse eyes, and under them were puffy bags that gave away his age. Virgile looked at the man's hands, speckled with liver spots, and saw that he was holding *La Terre*, the weekly farmer's communist-party newspaper. The old man nodded politely and headed toward the worn armchair that was close to the stove. He grimaced as he sank into the cushion. Evelyne had told Virgile that the cold exacerbated her father's arthritis, but he refused to let it slow him down.

"Did you know that our new boarder and Joachim share the same birthday? And Mr. Virgile played rugby, too. Isn't that a coincidence?"

Mr. Cantarel barely acknowledged her remark and opened up his paper.

"My father isn't very talkative," Evelyne said.

The next moment, a young man came running down the stairs. He was in a navy-blue sweat suit, a baseball cap on his head.

"So, there you are!" Evelyne exclaimed. "Let me introduce Virgile, our houseguest. You two have a lot in common."

Evelyne's effusion made Virgile feel uncomfortable. He put out a strong and sincere hand to this Joachim. Although he was not very chatty, the Cantarel son soon warmed up. Before long they were talking about rugby, the Bayonne festivals, Pamplona, the Armagnac that was no longer selling very well, Joachim's recent job as a volunteer firefighter in Saint-Justin, and then, of course, girls. Joachim apparently was in love, but he didn't have much to say about this, as it wasn't a subject that was discussed under the family roof.

Evelyne went to the kitchen and returned with four dishes, which she set on the oilcloth-covered table. Of course Virgile would stay for the meal. "I was sure you two would become thick as thieves," Evelyne said happily as she filled two shot glasses with a dark and murky but deliciously scented liquid.

"It's walnut liqueur, homemade!" Evelyne said, loosening the cap of the relic-like vial.

The menu that followed confirmed the culinary talents of the former Château Blanzac servant. Pan-fried duck liver, stuffed goose neck, arugula salad, and flakey apple pastries made up this "simple" meal, so called by the creator of the feast. She claimed that she had thrown it together. Virgile, who had just finished eating at Au Trou Gascon, didn't know how he could eat any more, but the food on this table was too tempting. He dug in.

Then they lingered over eau-de-vies from Bas Armagnac: Domaine Boignières, Domaine Roger Luquet, Domaine d'Espérance, and, natu-rally, Château de Briat.

The elder Cantarel went upstairs, and after clearing up, Evelyne retired to her own room. With the help of the brandy, the two young men discovered that they had even more in common. Joachim had been drawn to oenology himself. He didn't have the money to study in Bordeaux or Montpellier, though, so he had accepted a job as warehouseman in the nearby township of Le Houga. It didn't pay well, but at least he could stay in the area. At any rate, his mother wouldn't hear of his moving away. He dreaded the day he would have to tell her that he was in love and wanted to marry. He was eager to have a home and life of his own.

"And what about your father?" Virgile asked hesitantly.

"What, my father?" Joachim said. "He took off the day he found out my mother was pregnant. A son-of-a-bitch, that guy! The closest thing I've ever had to a dad is my grandfather."

"But your mother never told you anything about your dad?"

"Never."

"Why?"

"I don't know. All I can say is that as soon as my mother got pregnant, her troubles began. The Castayracs fired her that year, and my grandmother died. She's been single her whole life."

"She never wanted to marry or have a serious relationship with any other man?" Virgile asked, realizing that he was venturing close to the line.

"No, she always said that two men in the house—my grandfather and me—were enough.

At least I don't think she ever loved anyone else. Well, yes, maybe…"

Joachim wrapped his oversized hands around the nearly empty glass of Armagnac. He was holding it too tight. Virgile looked up and saw that his new friend's eyes had taken on a steely hue.

"You have suspicions?"

"I think, when she was very young, she had a crush on Francisco, the Castayracs' cellar master. Anyway, we have those bastards to thank for our problems."

"And what if Francisco was your father?"

"Stop talking bullshit! Why do you say that?"

"Simple hypothesis."

The glass broke, and blood gushed over Joachim's fingers. But instead of letting go, he began to squeeze the glass shards, driving them into his hand. He stared at Virgile, the veins in his neck bulging. Then, to Virgile's horror, he rammed his head into the glass. Witnessing Joachim's self-mutilation, Virgile sprang into action and put him in a judo hold, preventing him from harming himself any further. Now on the floor, Joachim could not overpower Virgile. He surrendered. His breathing became more regular. Color returned to his cheeks. His eyes lost their deathly fixedness, and his mouth began to tremble. Virgile let go and grabbed a kitchen towel, which he soaked in Armagnac and dabbed on the cuts. Despite all the blood, they looked relatively minor. Virgile heaved a sigh of relief. No stitches needed. He had repeated the first aid that Valmont had administered to him that very morning. Decidedly, in Armagnac country, the truth cut like a knife!

Joachim gave his rescuer a weak smile. When, little by little, he recovered his senses and he stammered a few awkward words of excuse.

"Francisco used to take me in his arms when I was little, on Sundays, when we picnicked with Mom by the Douze River. But he never was man enough to admit it and take his responsibilities. Mom won't talk about it. But you don't even know me. What made you say that?"

"I'm a Virgo, like you," Virgile said, patting him on the shoulder. "We know how to put two and two together."

7

The Labradors announced his arrival as Benjamin approached the door. The sporting dogs quickly quieted, and Benjamin hadn't even touched the bronze knocker on the Blanzac door when Lord Castayrac pulled it open and greeted him with a cold and mocking laugh.

"I was convinced, Mr. Wine Expert, that you wouldn't come tonight."

"To be honest, I thought the same thing after your friends elected Aymeric de Nadaillac chairman of the committee."

"No one can betray us like family!"

"You must admit, the events of the past month didn't help you."

"You don't know me very well. I'll make a comeback. Mark my words!"

"Mr. Castayrac, you're talking like a casino gambler, which you are, I believe." Benjamin said this with a dash of provocation.

"On occasion. Life is a perpetual gamble, isn't it, Mr. Cooker?"

"Yes, indeed it is, but you still have to have the means to bet!" Benjamin rubbed it in. Castayrac hadn't offered to hang up Benjamin's Loden, but he took it off anyway and slipped it onto a hook. The winemaker intended to let the man know that civility and stonewalling would no longer set the tone for their visits.

As he had predicted, the aristocrat was intoxicated. The man smelled of whiskey and Virginia tobacco. With an unsteady hand, he pointed the way to the library. Benjamin already knew the way, as well as the contents of this room. Leather-bound books on natural history on the left, close to the door. Books on agronomy on the upper-right shelves. Toward the back, the Carrara marble fireplace and the two thin andirons. On the mantel, the gilt bronze clock, forever silenced.

The room was even colder than usual. Benjamin took a seat on the faded gold sofa with threadbare fringe. Facing him on the pedestal table was the photograph of Elise de Castayrac, maiden name Riquet de Lauze. Even with that smug look on her face, the photo gave the fusty surroundings a touch of humanity.

"Mr. Castayrac, the initial findings my assistant and I have gathered are significantly different from the figures you suggested this morning."

"So you're calling me a liar," the baron said as he pulled the stopper off a large decanter of whiskey.

The flask, sitting on a nested table whose marquetry had suffered a few poorly extinguished cigars, was largely depleted.

Castayrac continued. "Bourbon?"

"No, thank you."

"Gin, then?"

"Just Armagnac," the winemaker said, close to becoming exasperated.

Castayrac walked to the other end of the room and disappeared down the steps leading to his private reserve. Benjamin figured he had quite a few vintage Armagnacs down there.

"Nineteen eighty-six? Will that do?"

"Perfect! That's the year Simone de Beauvoir died," Benjamin said.

"I don't go in much for trivia."

"Is that so? Or women's rights, either. That's also the year you dispensed with Miss Cantarel's services. But perhaps that was not your decision, but rather your wife's?" Philippe and Beatrice had already told Benjamin the story, and he planned to use the information to his advantage.

"I don't see the connection to the matter at hand," Castayrac said, giving Benjamin his glass of Armagnac.

"There isn't any, I assure you," Benjamin replied, warming the glass with his hands. "Unless…"

"Unless what?" Castayrac grumbled. "I don't like your insinuations, Mr. Cooker. Come right out and say what you're thinking!"

"In Labastide, it was common knowledge that your cellar master had a relationship that was rather…passionate, shall we say, with…"

"With?" the baron exclaimed, emptying his glass in one gulp. Then, looking away from Benjamin, he answered the question himself. "With my wife!"

Benjamin hoped this admission would be the first of many. The Armagnac—plus the alcohol consumed before Benjamin's arrival—was loosening the baron's tongue. Castayrac, clumsy in the darkness, started pacing the room and mumbling half-sentences.

The winemaker refrained from taking notes. Now and then, he clicked his tongue, enjoying the candied-orange flavors of the eau-de-vie and lingering aromas from the time spent in oak barrels. Francisco's blendings were truly fine. The fellow must have been terribly in love that year.

"All that is ancient history. I forgave my wife before she took her last breath," the baron said, looking furious.

"That was the least you could do. You yourself were not above reproach."

"I will not allow you to talk that way."

"You're right. It's not for me to pass judgment on your private life. And yet I do believe that in the past you have often mixed business with pleasure."

"What's your point?"

"You gave me your word this morning that there were sixty demijohns in the cellar. However, we found evidence of only nineteen. So it seems that you weren't being honest with me. Perhaps you disposed of some of your liquid assets before the fire, without declaring the proceeds."

"Why would I do that?"

"To pay off gambling debts, I would think. It seems that Lady Luck abandoned you long ago, Mr. Castayrac."

The man collapsed in his Voltaire chair and poured himself another glass of the 1986 eau-de-vie.

"So I guess you consider me a terrible crook."

"It's a working hypothesis. Nothing more, nothing less."

Jean-Charles de Castayrac took two gulps of his old Armagnac and threw the rest into the fire. Instantly, the hearth lit up. Shadows played on the library shelves, and a delicious scent of grilled orange peel rose in the air.

The man's stooped shoulders and dangling arms cut a pitiful profile. It had been a rough day, and the baron's reputation had come out besmirched. The oldest member of the Castayrac family seemed to be on the road to ruin. The fleurs-de-lis and blue blood mattered little. Now, whatever the cost, he needed to wrest a few pennies from the insurance company and save what he could.

Castayrac pulled himself together and rummaged in the wood basket for a log substantial enough to keep some flames going, and then he tried a smokescreen.

"I haven't led the life you imagine, Mr. Cooker."

"I don't imagine anything, dear sir! I observe. I listen. I keep records if I can gather sufficient information, and then I send my report to the Protection Insurance. I must say you're not helping me get to the bottom of this."

"What do you want me to say? Yes, I sold some demijohns under the table. It was to pay for maintenance on the château and certainly not to…"

He stopped talking and looked at Benjamin, who had picked up his notebook again. Was Castayrac about to try a new tack? Sure enough, the baron began talking about his unfaithful wife and unhappy marriage.

"All my problems began when my wife became unfaithful to me. To think that she was cheating on me with that Spaniard Francisco!"

"I thought you trusted him implicitly."

"Yes, of course, up until the day I found out. Francisco had gotten involved with the Cantarel girl. When my wife discovered that he had cheated on her—with someone younger and prettier, no less—she immediately fired the good woman, who, of course, had no idea why."

"So the father of Evelyne Cantarel's son was none other than your cellar master?"

"It's hardly a secret. All of Labastide knows, except the boy himself. His mother is as silent as the grave. She's the perfect daughter-mother figure that you see so often in the countryside. When my wife died, I thought about rehiring her, but I couldn't bring myself to do it."

"Why not?"

"I don't know. Maybe because of my own sons. I wanted to show a modicum of respect for their mother. I had put all that behind us, and I wanted to keep it there."

"Did she have other lovers?" Benjamin asked, pouring himself a bit more of this 1986 spirit, which more than twenty-five years of aging had mellowed perfectly.

"The Cantarel girl?"

"No, your wife."

"Mr. Cooker, I am familiar with your expertise in the area of wine. I did not know you were so knowledgeable about affairs of the heart."

"Heartbreak, sir, is your best defense."

The Blanzac nobleman poked at his fire. He added another thick block of wood. This generosity was a far cry from the cold hearth he offered earlier. Perhaps he was trying to arouse some sympathy. Castayrac leaned against the mantel, his eyes riveted on the black-and-white picture of the descendant of the famed Alvignac waters. Her fleshy lips—the lips that had known so well how to kiss—seemed painted in bold brushstrokes.

"You were witness this morning to the contentious relationship that I have with my older son, Alban. He's a schemer, and he's arrogant. Thank goodness he married rather well, even though I'm still waiting for a grandchild. You know, sir, he's not a Castayrac."

The confession was both terse and pompous. It wasn't tinged with any remorse, just a hint of fatalism that gave the man a sort of nobility. His wife had sinned, but in the Castayrac family, reputation trumped conventional morality.

Some embers landed on the rug and began to burn the worn wool fibers. Castayrac crushed them under his heel. After a long sigh, he continued in a lower voice.

"Alban's father was a Bordeaux wine trader for Martinique. He saw to it that our Armagnacs crossed the Atlantic safely. He had become a sort of family friend, almost like a relative. I don't need to draw you a picture. He died of pancreatic cancer a few years after my wife."

"Does your son suspect anything?" Benjamin asked, shifting in his weight on the sofa and feeling a bit uncomfortable with these disclosures.

"Not in the least! And allow me to ask, my dear friend, for your complete discretion."

Benjamin nodded to show the request had been granted.

The baron cleared his throat and looked more humble now. No longer churlish and haughty, he started talking again.

"I raised him as my own son, and I am very disappointed that he is pouring his invaluable talents into Aymeric de Nadaillac's eau-de-vie. But can I blame him? Maybe I wasn't a good father. Do you have children, Mr. Cooker?"

"Yes, a daughter."

"I would have loved to have a daughter..."

Jean-Charles de Castayrac's eyes were brimming with tears. Benjamin found this display of emotion both pathetic and distasteful. He got up and started walking toward the shelves of old dictionaries in brown leather bindings.

His cell phone stopped him.

"Excuse me," Benjamin said, pulling out the phone. It was Philippe. "Hello, Philippe. Yes, please expect me for dinner, as planned."

From the corner of his eye Benjamin could see that the baron was paying close attention.

"Of course, Benjamin, we're looking forward to seeing you this evening," Philippe said. "But I'm also calling with some news. Aymeric de Nadaillac has just died in a car accident. He was driving from Gabarret. Black ice, they think."

Stunned, Benjamin ended the call and looked at the baron. "Mr. Castayrac, you've just lost a rival: Aymeric de Nadaillac. He's dead."

8

During the night, the wind from Spain had chased away the blanket of frost that had cloaked the vines and woods of Armagnac for three days. "We're in for some rain," Philippe de Bouglon had announced. His weather predictions were never challenged. He could read the sky the same way he could read the color of his Armagnacs. "When you come down to it, the weather is simply a matter of blending: hot and cold uncontrollably subjected to air pressure," he had joked, smoothing the russet-colored moustache that sometimes gave him the look of an Irish whiskey merchant.

It was just past seven now, and Benjamin was on his way to the Cantarel house to rouse Virgile. Surely Mrs. Cantarel would offer him tea, or at least a steaming cup of coffee. The very thought of it inspired him to quicken his pace.

Two black cats were vying for turf in Labastide-d'Armagnac's deserted Place Royale, where Benjamin parked the car. A figure shrouded in a scarf slipped out of view as the winemaker passed by. Benjamin heard a lock click, ending any chance of conversation. Then the winemaker, a lover of old stones, stood in the middle of the square and studied the vaulted arcades, which were perfectly aligned along three sides of a quadrangle protected by a church tower. The village had changed very little since the sixteenth century. He thought of what his friend Philippe had told him: Henry the Fourth, who had visited Labastide-d'Armagnac several times, had used this square as his inspiration when he ordered the layout of the Place des Vosges in Paris. Perhaps it was just a legend or a bit of regional boasting, but Benjamin found the idea entirely believable. He was fond of these little encounters with French history, which, in the land of Aquitaine, had merged with that of Old England.

A yellow postal truck interrupted the peace and quiet. Bundled in a dark parka, the driver assessed Benjamin with suspicion and then gave him a nod. The medieval town was stirring.

Taking the Rue du Café-Chantant, the wine-maker imagined the private lives of the residents. Behind a few of the windows, the lace curtains were already pulled back. On the cobblestone street, a balding spaniel was searching for suste-nance in a ripped-open garbage bag. He trotted over to Benjamin and sniffed the winemaker's Loden. Benjamin gave the spaniel a pat on the head and continued on, glad that his own dog, Bacchus, didn't have to forage for food. Finally, he turned onto the Rue des Taillandiers, where he spotted the half-timber house. He walked up to it and knocked on the door.

"Already here, boss?" Virgile said, sitting at the table with a cup of steaming coffee. Sitting next to him was a young man with a scratched face but lively, almost reckless expression.

With warmth that seemed natural, Evelyne Cantarel invited Benjamin to share their breakfast of plum jam, quince jelly, honey, fresh orange juice, and bread toasted to perfection. Benjamin did not need to be cajoled.

The conversation soon turned to Aymeric de Nadaillac's death. Edmond Cantarel, emerging from his silence, was both suspicious and stubborn. "It was no accident. You'd have a hard time convincing me otherwise."

"Papa, stop that nonsense!" his daughter reproached, pouring a stream of strong black coffee into Benjamin's white porcelain cup with gold trim. "Car accidents happen all the time. Maybe he was worried or tired. I don't know. In any case, things will work out for the Castayracs."

"You'll see. Those bastard wine producers will make Castayrac their chairman, even though he doesn't have a drop of Armagnac in his blood. Don't you think so?" Grumbling, the patriarch took a seat at the end of the table.

Benjamin, put on the spot, nodded as he smeared quince jelly on his toast.

"Indeed, I'm afraid your prediction is probably correct."

"You see, Evelyne, even the gentleman here thinks the way I do!" said Cantarel. He raised his glass of red wine to toast them.

"Here's to your health! Nothing in the morning like a glass of good wine, a slice of Bayonne ham, duck rillettes, and country bread. Real bread, not some Parisian baguette for weaklings! No, a real round loaf with a crust that sticks to your ribs. Because, sir, woodcock hunting ends today. There's no time to waste, and lying in wait all day long makes you hungry," the old man said, slipping the blade of his Laguiole knife into the bread and cutting himself another slice.

Ignoring his grandfather, as well as Benjamin, Joachim gave Virgile a mischievous look. "I think you're on the wrong track, my friends. It's not the baron who'll be elected. It's the Nadaillac son-in-law. Just wait. The election will end up being between the Castayrac father and son. There will be blood."

"Why do you say that?" Virgile asked.

"You'll see. I have a hunch."

"That's a clever notion, sonny!" said old Cantarel.

Benjamin observed this exchange with interest. He was feeling so cozy in the warmth of this household, he could almost make coffee his exclusive morning drink.

"I see all the coffee's gone," Evelyne said. "I'll make some more."

"That's very nice of you, but please don't go to the trouble," Virgile said. He had already left the table with Joachim, who was checking his watch.

"I'm outta here," Joachim said. "Will I see you later, Virgile?"

Virgile agreed to accompany his new friend to rugby practice later in the day, as long as his employer didn't object.

"On one condition," Benjamin said. "That you don't spend the whole match on the bench, and no celebrating afterward. You know what I mean!"

A wink between the two young men and a smile from the winemaker sealed the deal.

The winemaker would have gladly prolonged the breakfast conversation, but Joachim was gone, and Cantarel was busy getting ready for the hunt. The woodcocks would not wait. Cantarel put on his winter coat, took down his Browning rifle from the gun rack, clipped on his cartridge belt, and headed to the door.

"Anyway, when it comes to those two, one is as bad as the other," the old man concluded. He whistled to his hunting dog, who turned out to be none other than the spaniel Benjamin had seen foraging in the village street.

When the winemaker and his assistant left the Cantarel house for Château Blanzac, the weathervane on the church was spinning. The wind was blowing from Landes, and the dark sky in the west was confirming Philippe de Bouglon's prediction.

§ § §

The rest of the day brought little new information. Virgile sifted through the debris of the charred wine cellar, counting and recounting the cask hoops, as well as the necks of the broken demijohns, but his conclusions were unchanged. The estimates and calculations were significantly lower than what the baron had submitted on his insurance claim.

After a heavy lunch at an inn in Mauvezind'Armagnac, Benjamin slipped into his room at Château Prada, determined to work on his report. This could only be accomplished, of course, if his friend didn't try to distract him with an on-the-spot tasting of the robust and fiery eau-de-vie straight from the still. He would never be able to resist temptation if Philippe appeared at his door with vials wafting fragrances of pear, plum, and lime.

In fact, Benjamin Cooker didn't write more than two lines of his report that afternoon, as the call of the mouthwatering Blanche d'Armagnac, with its finesse and irresistible aromas, was too powerful. It got the better of both Benjamin and

Philippe. The two ended the evening slouched in their armchairs. Feeling bawdy, they took turns recalling the women they had romanced in their youth. On occasion, they had even gone after the same girl.

"Those were the days," Philippe said, his eyes glassy.

"Yes, but these days are better, my friend," Benjamin responded. He smiled and closed his eyes. "Who would have thought we'd end up with such fine wives? 'There is only one happiness in life, to love and be loved.'"

"George Sand."

"Correct you are," Benjamin said. Then the look of bliss left his face and he sat up. "But the goings on in Labastide bring to mind Jean-Paul Sartre: 'Commitment is an act, not a word.' That is a lesson lost on some."

§ § §

The strong smell of camphor floated through the Cazaubon stadium locker room. Several players had suffered bumps and bruises, and the trainer, a puny loud-mouthed guy with agile fingers, was busy massaging calves and shoulders that ached from the blows. Joachim and Virgile had emerged unscathed from the practice match against the

Villeneuve-de-Marsan team. Despite the minor injuries, the Cazaubon players were said to be invincible.

"Shit, you guys play like animals!" the former wing of the Bergerac rugby team teased his friend as he came out of the shower.

"Friendly game or championship match, it makes no difference. Show no mercy! But you play awfully well for someone who hasn't touched a ball in a few years," Joachim replied.

Virgile grinned.

The Cazaubon coach appraised Virgile with the eye of a horse trader. "Is your pal from around here?" he said, looking at Joachim. "Think he'd like to play for us?"

"Ask him yourself, but I don't think we could afford him," the striker said, sounding mysterious.

Virgile, with a towel around his waist, pretended not to hear. The man in the sweat suit put a hand on his shoulder and made the offer in a tone meant to be polite.

"Too bad, but I just signed with Toulouse," Virgile answered without blinking.

"Oh, really?" the coach said, taken aback. "And what's your name?"

"Galthié. Virgile Galthié. The cousin of the one you've heard of. Yes, that one, the former captain of the national rugby team."

The Cazaubon coach looked stunned and turned to Joachim. "When you have friends like that, let me know," he said in a hushed voice. "And don't waste any time."

As soon as the coach had turned his back, the two accomplices grinned at each other, trying hard to suppress their laughter.

In keeping with his agreement, Virgile didn't engage in any post-game celebrating. He settled for a bock beer at the Café de la Poste. This gave Joachim the opportunity to introduce his teammate for a day to his heartthrob, a slender brunet beauty. Her name was Constance.

As soon as he saw her green eyes and graceful figure, Virgile knew he was in trouble. Obviously, he couldn't compromise his new friendship. So he decided to call it a night and go back to Labastide. He was tired from the match, anyway. But he had a hard time banishing the vision of Joachim's girlfriend from his brain, and he slept fitfully.

9

The Estang church was too small to accommodate the crowd at Aymeric de Nadaillac's funeral service. But Father Péchaudoux, addressing the confined assembly in coats reeking of mothballs and dried lavender, was clearly in his element, and the Mass went on and on. The priest's voice rose to the rafters as he swept from one part of the liturgy to the next.

"Receive, oh Lord, into your kingdom your servant Aymeric, who, during his life on earth, never ceased working with determination, devotion, and selflessness for the good of the vineyards."

Behind a dark veil, the Nadaillac widow stared at the coffin through the entire service. Looking dignified in black, her daughter and son-in-law worshipped at her right.

When the pipe organ started playing the majestic recessional hymn, the pallbearers picked up the oak coffin and began walking down the center aisle. The family followed. As the casket passed each pew, the men lifted their berets and bowed before the remains of the last of the great figures of the farmers trade union.

Once the mourners were outside the church, though, the gossip started. Everyone was speculating on Nadaillac's successor as head of the Armagnac Promotion Committee, and there was hardly any agreement.

"The son-in-law will definitely make a run for it," some said.

"Don't be stupid. Old Castayrac has the election wrapped up," others predicted.

From a distance, Benjamin watched Jean-Charles de Castayrac. He was wearing an appropriately solemn expression. But privately, Castayrac had to be gloating. With Nadaillac out of the way, his election as committee chairman was in the bag.

Benjamin stood beside Philippe and Beatrice de Bouglon at the cemetery. As was the tradition in Gascony, everyone threw a handful of earth on the coffin before making the sign of the cross. The winemaker followed suit and extended his condolences to the family at the cemetery gate. He was taken aback to see Alban de Castayrac refuse his father's embrace. An awkward moment followed, causing a stir in the crowd. Likewise, the widow and her daughter refused to shake the baron's hand.

Seeing this scene play out, Benjamin wondered if Castayrac realized at that exact moment that his oppositional son was, indeed, dead serious about challenging him for the chairmanship of the committee. If so, the owner of Château Blanzac didn't show it. "My thoughts are with you," he told the widow before moving along.

Just then, a gust of wind lifted Mrs. de Nadaillac's veil. Benjamin wasn't surprised to see that her eyes were clear, and no mascara was running down her cheeks.

§ § §

The next day, when Benjamin slid the large manila envelope into the mailbox outside the post office, he knew his report would send shock waves through Protection Insurance. Benjamin's reservations were numerous, explicitly formulated, and thoroughly substantiated. Once again the winemaker from Bordeaux had demonstrated his expertise. In his detailed account, he had gone to great lengths to prove that the baron's claim differed significantly from the Cooker & Co. inventory. Even with a five to ten percent margin of error, the damage estimate was far less than what the injured party had claimed. Benjamin wrote in his conclusions:

Jean-Charles de Castayrac has admitted that a portion of the reserves stored in his Château Blanzac wine cellar was secretly disposed of before the December 24 fire. Given that admission, I would recommend consulting the Directorate-General of Customs and Indirect Taxes. Of course, the decision to initiate such action remains with your company. It would certainly have serious consequences for your client, who now heads the Armagnac Promotion Committee.

In reference to the appraisal performed at the site, it is highly likely that the maximum loss incurred by the claimant, Mr. Castayrac, is on the order of seventy-five hundred liters, of which barely ten percent could be considered centenarian. Based on the rate approved by the joint-trade association of Armagnac, the compensation should be approximately...

Benjamin had to literally stuff the envelope into the already-full mailbox. This was just a formality, though, as he had sent it by e-mail the day before. The insurance agents were probably already reading it.

Just as he was about to walk away, the baron's DS made a swift U-turn on the Promenade des Embarrats. Jean-Charles de Castayrac waved to the winemaker as he emerged from the car. The Blanzac owner wasn't a humble victor. He was swaggering. The board of directors of the Armagnac Promotion Committee had wasted no

time electing him chairman that very morning—
by a very large majority.

Before returning to Château Prada, Benjamin
decided to lose himself one more time in the
walled town of proud half-timber houses and
gleaming cobblestones. He was tempted to light
up a Lusitania but decided against it. His mind
was troubled. He didn't acknowledge Beatrice
and Philippe de Bouglon's kids as they passed
him, squabbling, on their way home from school.

Lost in thought, the winemaker quickened his
pace toward what looked, in the distance, like an
ancient washhouse. When he got there, he saw
that it was nothing more than a concrete basin
holding stagnant water. Beautiful washerwomen
and their hearty peals of laughter were just a
memory of times long gone. Nostalgic and per-
turbed, Benjamin stared at the duckweed floating
gently on a thick layer of sludge.

The following day, he would leave behind the
Bouglons' hospitality and this fortified town as old
as the Armagnac in its moldy wine cellars. In the
end, he hadn't been able to crack the secret of this
land, where vineyards vied with oak trees for su-
premacy. Listless and without any appetite, he was
heading toward the château by way of the Rue
des Pas-Perdus and the Rue des Fossés when he
spotted Virgile and Joachim hurrying toward him.

"Boss, I was taking one last look around the wine cellar at Blanzac, and I found something that looked suspicious."

Joachim, who hadn't even said hello, seemed to be breathing heavily. And his face looked tense.

"Too late, my boy. My report is already in the mail. Virgile, you know what I think of the baron. I don't believe I have anything more to say about the man's integrity."

"I know, boss. He's a small-time crook in your eyes. But what if he were a serious criminal?"

Benjamin was skeptical, but he would hear his assistant out. He reached for the double Corona in his coat pocket. Using his teeth, he severed the head of the cigar and lit the Havana. The nutty-smelling twenty centimeters seemed to disturb Joachim, who was wordlessly observing the scene. Virgile said nothing for a few seconds. He was familiar with this lighting ritual. The winemaker always insisted on a second puff to fully experience his cigar before he was ready to listen.

"Near the still that exploded, I found this in the ashes."

Benjamin put on his reading glasses and studied the piece of metal that Virgile had pulled from his pocket. It was barely two inches long and looked like a tube with a melted rod on top. It bore the stamp SGDG.

"So? This is your discovery?" Benjamin said, handing the object back to his assistant. "It's one of the valves that connect the still's coils to the manometer. It's used to check the vapors."

"That's what you think!" Virgile responded, an excited look in his eyes. "You agree, boss, that it's made of brass?"

Benjamin looked at the object again and nodded.

"But we both know that all the components of an Armagnac still are made of copper."

"That's true," Benjamin said. He wanted to hear more.

"This is actually a butane lighter—a nickel-plated brass lighter."

"Look, sir," Joachim said, grabbing the piece of metal. "It has a tax seal."

"Yes, boss," Virgile said. "From 1911 to 1945, the '*Ministere Finances*' seal was required on practically all lighters. And every lighter manufacturer had to pay for the seal."

"How do you know this?" Benjamin asked.

"My grandfather Armand," Virgile said, clearly eager to continue his explanation. "Anyway, the government has always made money off smokers. When you buy your cigars, how much of the price do you think the Treasury Department gets?"

"Too much," Benjamin replied tersely.

"Three quarters, boss!"

"Virgile, you seem to know a lot about this subject."

"The drawers at my grandfather's house in Montravel were full of lighters. When I was a kid, Grandpa would sometimes let me light up the undergrowth. We were doing slash and burn, and we didn't even know it."

With a twist of the wrist, Joachim unscrewed the base of the lighter. The fuel reservoir was no larger than a thimble.

"Okay," Benjamin said. "We've got an old lighter here. It's quite a leap, however, to say that this proves Castayrac is a criminal. I admire your enterprise, Virgile, but you'll have to do more to persuade me."

Virgile fell silent and looked at his friend, whose face still looked full of tension. Benjamin's cigar was glowing brightly now, the wind from the west having picked up considerably.

"Well, go ahead. Tell him," Virgile insisted.

"It's odd," Joachim stammered. "But I'm certain that Francisco—I mean my father—never smoked."

"Are you sure?"

"I swear to God!" Joachim said. He was getting more agitated.

"That complicates matters," Benjamin said, sensing the young man's anger. He instinctively reached out and put a fatherly hand on Joachim's shoulder.

"That bastard wanted to burn down his cellars, and he killed my dad in the process! First he fires my mom, then he kills my dad. I'll make that son of a bitch Castayrac pay. I'll kill him, just like he killed my father!"

Night had already fallen, and Joachim let out a howl for all the world to hear. It was the pain of a wounded and humiliated child. Alarmed dogs all around began barking, and Benjamin heard nearby shutters slam shut. Moaning, Joachim started running away. Virgile tried to catch him, but the nimble athlete disappeared under the arches of the Place Royale and slipped into the darkness.

Virgile gave Benjamin a helpless look.

"How dangerous is he, boy?"

"He's hurt, a bit emotional, but honestly, I don't think he'd hurt a fly."

"Go back to the Cantarels and wait for Joachim to return. I'll drive around and see if I can spot him."

After an hour of searching, in vain, Benjamin took out his cell phone and called the local police to tell them about the brass lighter and the hot-headed kid. When he mentioned the name Castayrac, the desk officer informed him that a team was already at Château Blanzac.

Crossing the Place des Ormeaux, Benjamin Cooker called home to tell Elisabeth that he would have to stay even longer. He heard her sigh, and he apologized. He would make it up to her. Right now he had to be where he was. Blanzac was far from revealing all its secrets, and he was sure now that the findings in his report were null and void.

§ § §

As Benjamin drove up to Château Blanzac, he noted someone standing in a round attic window. Stiff and impassive, Valmont, the second son, was looking down on the courtyard. Indeed, it was a very odd spectacle. A procession of unmarked police cars, along with a van, was spread out on the château grounds. He parked and got out of his Mercedes.

Men in midnight-blue sweaters were quick to order Lord Castayrac to lower his voice. Certainly, this was his home, and he could boast the grandiose title of chairman of the Armagnac Promotion Committee, cry out in protest, and single-handedly represent the entire lot of regional producers, but that did not change the fact that the public prosecutor of Mont-de-Marson had issued a search warrant on behalf of the Directorate-General of Customs and Indirect Taxes.

The orchestrator of this lightning intervention, sturdy and hopelessly bald, was an educated man, and he intended to let the suspect know it.

"Lord Castayrac—since this is how you prefer to be addressed—your nobility does not put you above the law. I believe your assistance could be interpreted as a form of voluntary cooperation in our search for the truth. That's in our mutual interest, is it not?"

The owner of Blanzac stopped resisting the inevitable. "Then go ahead, gentlemen. Search the whole place. But what exactly am I accused of?"

Meanwhile, the officers were calling to each other. "Hey, Chief!" "This too, Chief?" "Look, Captain!"

In the bustle, Benjamin had walked into the library, where he was met with gaping closet doors and heaps of ripped-open files. Bank statements and paperwork of every kind were strewn all over the floor.

Benjamin took a deep breath. This was his doing. Protection Insurance was living up to its name. The company had evidently agreed with his conclusions and suspected insurance fraud, as well as tax fraud stemming from the baron's covert sale of his Armagnac. The lighter would add another charge with consequences that were much more serious for the ruined aristocrat: destruction of property leading to unintentional death.

Castayrac's bathrobe, made of fine wool from the Pyrenees, was thrown over the back of the sofa. Benjamin just stood there, until he heard gravel crunching in the courtyard, car doors slamming, and engines starting. Then nothing. As he turned to leave, he saw Valmont in the doorway, silent, with tears running down his face. He wouldn't be seeing his father again anytime soon.

Even the Bouglons' warmth and Beatrice's truffle omelet would not be enough to hearten Benjamin that evening.

§ § §

The next day the Saint-Justin Police Department received a second missing person's report. Alban de Castayrac, after his crushing defeat in the race for chairman of the committee, had not been seen since the election. His wife was worried sick, and his mother-in-law was praying to Saint Rita. It was said that both of them were inconsolable. Some residents spoke of suicide; others, in greater numbers, suspected he had run off because of a love affair gone sour.

But it was Joachim Cantarel's disappearance that worried Benjamin and Virgile. Both of them were aware of the fragile mental state of this great big fellow who fired up the crowds in the stadiums of Gascony.

Evelyne Cantarel was overcome with worry. Trying to be useful, her father started organizing a search in the surrounding woods. Joachim's teammates were distressed, too. Cazaubon was scheduled to play the team from Hagetmau later in the week, and Joachim needed to show up. The first place in the Aquitaine league was at stake.

That night, a noise in the attic awakened Virgile. He held his breath. Had birds gotten in through a hole in the chimney? Then he heard other noises. Footsteps, muffled conversation, someone carefully shutting the attic door. Between the rumpled sheets, Virgile sensed heavy breathing in the hallway, near the stairs. He slipped out of his bed and quietly cracked his door. He watched as two shadows slipped down the stairs. The front door opened.

Now Virgile sprang into action—but not to shoo the pair out of the house. He wanted to make sure the second figure didn't get away. It was Joachim. Even in the dark, Virgile could see his emotional exhaustion. Virgile grabbed Joachim before he could take another step and dragged him to his bedroom. He ordered his friend to be quiet and lie down. No talking, just sleep.

Virgile wrapped himself in a quilt and collapsed in a tattered armchair, trying to wedge himself between the least uncomfortable springs. He was not reassured until he heard the rugby player fall into a deep slumber. Virgile thought of Constance. Nothing shy about her! He had wondered if birds were nesting in the attic. And they were, all right. Lovebirds!

The aroma of Arabica coffee soon wrested him from his restless dozing.

Evelyne Cantarel burst into tears when she learned that her son was home. She hugged Virgile as if he were a godsend and told her story. Yes, she had loved Francisco. And yes, she had lured him away from La Riquette. She had no regrets. Francisco was a free spirit and they had never married, but he was the only man she had ever loved.

"Tell me, Mrs. Cantarel," Virgile asked when she had finished her disclosures. "Do you believe the baron started the fire in his wine cellar?"

"I don't know," she responded, staring at her cup of café au lait.

"Do you hold him responsible for Francisco's death?"

"Who knows? The baron could have been responsible. But maybe he wasn't. I believe in fate, Mr. Virgile. This might sound horrible, but maybe Francisco's death was just meant to be. Do you really think it was a criminal act?"

"I'm not the only one to think so, Mrs. Cantarel. Joachim is convinced, too."

"Castayrac is certainly a swindler, and he sold his Armagnac under the table, but I don't think he would burn down his own cellar to collect the insurance, even if he was broke. People around here also say that he had to take out a mortgage on the house. Do you believe that, Mr. Virgile?"

"Who might have wanted to start the fire, if not him?" Virgile pressed.

"Who knows? Maybe it was Alban," the woman ventured in a conspiratorial tone. "That father and son hate each other so much."

They heard footsteps on the stairs. It was Evelyne's father, rosy-cheeked and clear-eyed. He had dreamed that his grandson had come home.

"You're right, Papa! Joachim is sleeping like a baby in Mr. Virgile's room."

"What an idiot! And here I rounded up all the hunters in town to comb the woods."

"Stop carrying on like that. You'll make your blood pressure go up."

"But good God, where was he hiding?"

Virgile put on his most innocent face to absolve his friend. "In a deep thicket perfect for emptying a cartridge belt!"

Old Cantarel showed his missing teeth in a peal of laughter that rang through the house. On this morning, no one drinking the smooth Arabica coffee in the Cantarel kitchen would be reproaching Joachim.

10

After breakfast, Virgile showed up at Château Prada, looking for Benjamin. Beatrice Bouglon told Virgile that the news of the baron's arrest had spread through Labastide like wildfire. People all over town were expressing mixed feelings about the whole sad affair. Few were shedding tears for the baron, but some were feeling sad for Evelyne Cantarel. She had never married Francisco, but she had certainly lost the love of her life, and everyone knew it.

"Benjamin's off at the market," she concluded.

"If you see him, tell him I'm with Joachim," Virgile said before leaving with a little skip in his step.

§ § §

An even row of corpses, most of them covered in white, lined the shelves. Shopping bags at the ready, women in berets and woolen shawls lifted the cloth coverings to inspect the fowl, making sure there were no cuts or bruises. Plumpness was a priority, as well as an ample liver. Destined to be dismembered and cooked, the limp-necked ducks and geese practically implored the prospective buyers to put an end to their humiliating ordeal.

Despite the bitter cold, the Eauze market was teeming with noisy wildlife of the human kind. The morning meat market brought together people from all over the region. Benjamin was fond of this atmosphere of mysterious transactions, knowing smiles, euros quickly tucked into pockets, and handshake deals. It reminded him of the truffle markets in Lalbenque and Richerenches, gourmet pilgrimage sites. He loved to go to Lalbenque with Elisabeth. He wouldn't miss this tasty spectacle for anything in the world. It was more like horse trading than shopping.

In this bustling milieu, Benjamin came upon Alban de Castayrac, accompanied by his wife. So he had turned up. The Nadaillac son-in-law was strutting as if nothing had happened. His father was behind bars, and the APC had convened again that very morning to elect him chairman of the organization. There he was, shaking hands like a politician, plotting in a hushed tone with some of them, and gesturing dramatically with others. Alban de Castayrac knew how to work a crowd. Benjamin overhead snippets of his conversation, which ranged from the market value of

Armagnac to promised assistance from Brussels, which would curb the endemic crisis in the eau-de-vie trade. Jean-Charles de Castayrac's arrest and the resignation he was forced to submit a few hours thereafter had been quite convenient for Alban. Seeing him hold forth in this market, where he even slipped in some words in the local dialect, one couldn't help but wonder if the son had dealt his father's deathblow.

Alban de Castayrac walked toward the wine-maker. Benjamin knew it was more for the sake of courtesy than honest conversation.

"Still with us, Mr. Cooker? You must be very fond of Gascony!"

"You are fortunate, young man, to live in a part of the country that does not readily reveal itself. A person has to travel through it, sniff it, and tame it, in fact, to unlock all its mysteries. And heaven knows, everything is mysterious here. Don't you agree? Oh, by the way, congratulations on your election."

Alban took his wife by the elbow and melted into the crowd. Benjamin Cooker felt a little mischievous as he ambled toward a vendor selling hot chestnuts. Benjamin imagined that the man's face was just a bit anxious now and his handshake a tad weak.

The winemaker moved along, a warm paper cone in his hands. Seeing the ducks, he poked two or three with firm skin before settling on a fat specimen. The vendor, an old wizened woman, assured him that the liver weighed at least two pounds. Benjamin was trusting enough to take her word for it.

He decided to return to Médoc that morning. Virgile would stay on, but he missed Elisabeth, who had graciously put up with his prolonged absence. When he got there, he would light up the fireplace and slow-cook the duck in one of the large copper pots hanging above the sideboard in the kitchen. He'd do the work, and Elisabeth could just enjoy the warmth of the fire. The ensuing meal would be devilishly caloric, and a little heavy on the salt, but what could be more flavorful than confit? At the Cookers, a Crozes-Hermitage, a Madiran, a Cahors, or an excellent Gaillac would transform this gluttonous meal into a feast fit for a king.

§ § §

That very evening, Joachim, quicker and more agile than ever, attended rugby practice. He made two conversions and scored a fantastic goal. Virgile, however, was not permitted on the field. The Cazaubon coach had not appreciated his outrageous lie and intended to make him pay for it.

The people of Gascony weren't the type to forget. Virgile would have to make note of that, but he thought the coach was overdoing it and grumbled over not being able to play. His friend tried to console him at the Café de la Poste with a Maison Gélas vintage Armagnac. A few words from Constance would have lifted his spirits, but she only had eyes for her hero of the night. The first place in the Aquitaine championship was within reach. The Hagetmau players would be weak in the knees and shaking with fear. As proud as an Andalusian and as obstinate as a Castilian, Joachim was ready to take all bets. But his apparent enthusiasm could not conceal all the unanswered questions coming to light with the sudden fall of Castayrac Armagnac.

Francisco: so meticulous. There was no way in the world that he could have caused that fire. He had distilled at Blanzac year after year for more than a half-century. What about the lighter that no investigator had taken the trouble to examine, somehow assuming it was an archaic part of the Armagnac still? And how could this wise cellar master have been in the dark about his employer's multiple and repeated crimes of deception? All that eau-de-vie spirited away in order to pay off the carefree baron's gambling debts. Surely Francisco knew about it. His silence was as valuable as his blendings!

"Castayrac figured he could reduce the place to ashes and start all over again, like that bird that rises from the ashes," Joachim said.

"The phoenix," Virgile replied as they drove along the road from Cazaubon to Labastide. "The baron had to be desperate to do something so extreme." No sooner had he said this than a figure sprang up from the side of the road and leaped in front of the car. Joachim swerved just in time to miss him.

"Who was that nut?" Virgile shouted.

"Was he trying to get himself killed? Shit, the rush of adrenalin! Are you sure we didn't hit him?"

"Stop, Joachim. We'd better check."

The car came to a stop in the middle of nowhere. The beams from the headlights illuminated a stand of mossy oak trees and old bracken. The two athletes ran to the spot where they had seen the stranger. A nimble and graceful shadow finally rose up and quickly vanished into the fog-suffused woods.

"Forget about it, Joachim. He's a poacher. Look, he's running away like a rabbit."

"No, no," Joachim answered. "It's the Castayrac son Valmont. I'm sure of it. I'd bet my life on it."

"Come on, Joachim, you're seeing Castayracs all over the place!"

"No, Virgile. He has the eyes of a wolf. I'd recognize him anywhere."

"What's he doing around here at this hour?"

"I'm telling you, the whole family is crazy."

Once again, Virgile had trouble sleeping. To get at the truth, he had to figure out how to be as shrewd as his boss. Everything in Labastide, it seemed, was disturbing.

11

Virgile came through the gate at Château Prada just as the first glimmers of dawn were spilling over the countryside. Philippe de Bouglon, the only one awake at this hour, asked Virgile why he was up and about. Yes, he was a diligent and hard worker, but everyone needed a little sleep. Philippe had the bonhomie of people of the land who knew there was no need to rush in the winter. But he was unable to persuade the young assistant to go back to the Cantarels and get in another hour of sleep. So he offered Virgile some coffee. If he was going to be awake, he might as well be fully awake.

"I'm going to Blanzac," Virgile said after quickly downing the coffee. "I'll be back in an hour or two."

Virgile needed to satisfy his curiosity once and for all. Benjamin had often called him stubborn, and on that point the winemaker was entirely correct. Virgile didn't intend to let anything get in his way. He took off for Blanzac territory.

Only Athos and Aramis came to lick his hand. Porthos simply urinated copiously on the rear tire of the car he had borrowed from Joachim. He had an air of distrust punctuated by a licking of the chops. Virgile figured it was best to keep the dog at arm's length.

Virgile rapped on the door, but no human came to interrupt the dead silence of the place. Blanzac seemed abandoned. The winter cold re-inforced this impression of rust, seeping humidity, and snuffed-out nature. In the courtyard strewn with dead leaves, ceramic pots had broken in the icy weather. The lingering odor of wet ashes irritated Virgile's throat, as if the fire were still smoldering within the collapsed walls, where the charred staves and beams lay tangled in a heap of ghostlike blackness. Completing this macabre impression, an ashen mist shrouded the copper of the disembodied still. In Virgile's eyes, the prop-erty had never looked so sinister.

"Valmont? Valmont?" Virgile called out.

No answer. The countryside was without a sound.

Failing to get a response from the mansion, Virgile decided to have another look at the cel-lar. He had explored every square inch. He knew each bit of rubble, having exhumed, examined, evaluated, and quantified all of it. The explosion and resulting fire had spared nothing. Each strip of alcohol-soaked wood had been licked by the flames, roasted, and destroyed.

But once again he wandered into the rubble, kicking the muddy scraps of iron and wood as he poked through it. A thick lock was all that remained of the cellar door. He glanced at it—and looked again. Why on earth was the bolt engaged? Then it struck him. The cellar had been locked—from the outside! Francisco had never had a chance to escape. Joachim was right. His father had been murdered.

Virgile called his employer.

"Boss, sorry to disturb you, but you've got to hightail it back here. My apologies to Mrs. Cooker."

"What is it, son?"

"You'll see when you get here. And you'd better call the cops. I'm going to warm up at Prada. Call me when you get near. I'll meet you at Château Blanzac."

§ § §

As Benjamin got ready to leave Grangebelle, Elisabeth handed him cracklings for the Bouglons. She had carefully packaged the greasy treat in a small terrine covered with aluminum foil. Philippe and Beatrice were aware that Elisabeth's maiden name was Darrozière, a name redolent of the Gascony countryside and slow-cooked food. They would certainly appreciate this gift, even if it was as common as Armagnac in their region.

The winemaker had to return to Labastide-d'Armagnac anyway to collect Virgile, who had stayed behind. He was just leaving a little earlier than planned. The investigation for Protection Insurance was wrapped up, and Benjamin's conclusions had evidently unleashed the wrath of the law and the tax authorities. Nevertheless, Castayrac's precipitous fall troubled him, and he couldn't dismiss his doubts. Virgile, on the other hand, had no misgivings about the baron's culpability. Especially in light of his new friendship with Joachim, nothing would change his mind. Even that opportunist Alban found favor in his eyes.

§ § §

An hour and twenty-eight minutes later, the winemaker arrived at Château Blanzac with two reluctant-looking officers.

Benjamin turned to Virgile. "Well, what do you have to show us, Virgile?"

The assistant handed over his evidence. Benjamin examined it for a few moments and then gave it to the police officers. "It appears, gentlemen, that the cellar was locked from the outside."

From the beginning, the police—and just about everyone else in the region—had theorized that Francisco Vasquez's death was accidental.

"Considering Mr. Castayrac's reputation..." one of the officers stammered.

His fellow officer looked at Virgile and then at Benjamin.

"Mr. Cooker, will you authorize us to take credit for this crucial discovery by your invaluable colleague?"

"You need to ask him yourself. It isn't my decision to make," Benjamin grumbled.

Virgile shrugged. Although he felt like saying more, "yeah" was his only response.

The two officers walked over to their van, carefully took off their shoes, and pulled on khaki waders, which made them look ridiculous. They started searching for new clues in the charred debris.

With little to do, Benjamin tugged at Virgile's coat sleeve. "Come with me, Virgile. I can't resist stealing another look at the black Citroën DS hibernating at the back of the garage. I know you appreciate vintage cars too. After all, you have one yourself."

The Citroën was covered in canvas. Only the shiny hubcaps were visible. Virgile could tell that the winemaker's desire to slip into this sleek 1957

car—aerodynamic before its time—was irresistible. Benjamin started to lift the cover. Not one
second later, a beady-eyed Valmont de Castayrac
emerged from the shadows.

"I believe I already told you, Mr. Cooker. This
car is absolutely not for sale!"

Instantly, Virgile recognized the supple and robust figure, which the night before had appeared
ready to throw himself under the car.

§ § §

Benjamin slipped into the back of the public hearing room, hoping not to be noticed. Jean-Charles
de Castayrac kept proclaiming his innocence
and denouncing the plot against him. Brought
before the prosecutor, he cited his entire family
tree, the war records of his ancestors, and his
tireless battle to promote Armagnac throughout
the world as evidence of his good character. But
the Landes public prosecutor remained implaca-
ble. The baron's forebears and efforts on behalf
of Armagnac—which weren't selfless, because he
benefitted from them—did not make him a man
of virtue. Indeed, Castayrac had admitted his
bankruptcy, his chronic inability to manage his
property, and his weakness for gambling, society
life, and beautiful women. He also admitted to

the staggering amount of money he had taken from his in-laws before his wife's death to cover his abysmal losses from a deal gone bad.

"They were already so rich, sir, with their Alvignac spring water!" Castayrac had shouted.

To which the prosecutor responded, "You were just as rich from your own waters: eau-de vie!"

But the cavalier and frivolous behavior of the cynical baron wasn't what mattered most to the public servant. The baron had cheated the tax authorities, carried out insurance fraud, and, even more important, committed arson. His own cellar master had died in that fire.

"Does it take courage or heartlessness to set fire to one's own property?" the infuriated prosecutor had asked.

"But I am utterly incapable of that, sir."

"Incapable of love, yes. That I believe. You knowingly locked Francisco Valdez, the unfortunate man who had been faithful to your family for almost a half century, in your wine cellar before reducing it to ashes."

"I did nothing of the sort."

"Everyone knows that you had defaulted on your mortgage, and Crédit Agricole was planning to sell your estate at auction. Only the insurance payout could save you from disgrace."

"I admit I was in a bad situation, but good heavens, I never could have committed such an act!"

"Can you provide the slightest alibi to suggest that on December 24th you were not at Blanzac?"

The baron was quiet for a long time, as if he had run out of arguments.

"None," he finally said, running a weary hand through his hair. "Forgive me, sir, I don't feel very well."

"And for the very good and sole reason that I have put my finger where it hurts. Blanzac was going to be sold, and you were angry with your older son, the only one who could have helped you."

"Alban? You must be kidding! Him, help me? He never stopped humiliating me or prowling like a vulture around Blanzac to the point of trying to dispossess me. As recently as last week, he was my fiercest rival for the chairmanship of the APC! No, if you have to point the finger at someone, sir, you should be looking at him."

"I knew you were capable of many things," the prosecutor insisted, adjusting his glasses. "But with you, the worst is always yet to come. Incriminating your own son to clear your name! No one's buying it. You're providing enough rope to hang yourself. What interest would your offspring have had, no matter how ungrateful he was, to set your wine cellar ablaze? He's not the one who stood to collect the fat check from the insurance company. And why would he have done away with Francisco, as well? I believe the relationship between your cellar master and Alban was quite friendly."

"I cannot answer that question, sir. For all I know, his father-in-law was conspiring with the bank to buy the estate, and he planned to hand it over to Alban. Nadaillac would have gained control of one of his biggest competitors, and Alban would have been his own boss. My son never had many scruples."

"And neither do you, it appears."

With his head in his hands, Jean-Charles de Castayrac seemed to be trying to drown out the relentless accusations of the prosecutor. The light from the man's desk lamp illuminated the baron's signet ring. One could make out perfectly the Castayrac coat of arms: two unicorns and two matching trefoils.

"I believe we'll leave it at that for today," the prosecutor said, placing his pen in the white porcelain inkwell from another era.

The guards posted behind the suspect put their caps back on and got ready to leave. The hearing was over.

"When you feel the pangs of remorse, Mr. Castayrac, let me know. We'll save time that way. As uncomfortable as Château Blanzac may be, it's still warmer than our jails."

"Actually, I find your cell sufficiently comfortable, sir," the aristocrat answered, throwing his shoulders back.

"Lock him up until further notice," the prosecutor grumbled.

"Very well, sir," the first guard responded, taking the baron by the arm and leading him away. Benjamin noted that the prosecutor looked like an anachronism. His silk pinstriped suit looked like it was made by an eighty-year-old tailor. His bearing was pompous, and his voice was high-pitched.

§ § §

Back in his office, the prosecutor rose from his chair, walked over to the old cast-iron radiator, and warmed his hands while watching the van haul the fallen baron off to the old jail. Then he walked back to his Empire-style desk, picked up his telephone, and called the chief of police in Saint-Justin.

"Magistrate Canteloube here. I need you to do something for me. Pick up Alban Castayrac and bring him in. Right away."

§ § §

"With a father like that, I understand why Alban took off," Virgile told Benjamin during their lunch at Prada. "He would have married anyone to get away from Blanzac. It just happens that he made out rather well by marrying a Nadaillac."

"It seems to be a theme in the Castayrac family," Benjamin said. "The baron himself profited quite handsomely from his marriage."

Philippe and Beatrice de Bouglon were watching this exchange in silence. But after a few sips of a Henri Leroy Romanée-Conti, unearthed from the dark vaults of the Prada cellar, they added their own views. Philippe sided with Benjamin, who was having second thoughts about the whole matter, while Beatrice shared Virgile's opinion.

"There've always been rumors about the old man," Beatrice said. "Remember that underage girl? And the shadowy deals he's made—the people he's cheated. I wouldn't trust him for a minute."

"Beatrice, honey, hardly any of that stuff has ever been proved. It's talk. That's all."

"As far as I'm concerned, where there's smoke, there's fire!"

"In this particular case, my dear Bea, you couldn't be more right!" Benjamin burst into a hearty laugh, followed by Virgile and then Philippe de Bouglon, whose handsome musketeer moustache was glistening with duck-crackling grease.

The lunch was filled with racy stories about the baron and his wife. Tales of the couple's sexual antics—both factual and rumored—kept the four of them entertained to the last bite. La Riquette, the descendant of the famous Alvignac spring waters, wasn't one to forgive and forget. Betrayed by her frivolous husband, she had cheerfully given the baron a taste of his own medicine. Beatrice confirmed what the baron himself had confessed to Benjamin: Alban was the fruit of an adulterous relationship between Elise de Castayrac and a wine trader from Bordeaux, a "great friend of the family."

"And what about Valmont?" asked Virgile.

"As for the second son, they say he's the son of—"

Hearing a car pull into the château courtyard, the diners looked up. When the doorbell rang, Philippe de Bouglon wiped his moustache with the corner of his napkin as he rose from his chair to answer the doorbell. "Could we possibly have lunch in peace someday?"

The winemaker heard an exchange of polite greetings in the Prada entryway. "Benjamin, it's for you!" Philippe called out.

Who would be looking for him? He gave Virgile and Beatrice an inquisitive look. Shrugging, he took another sip of his Romanée-Conti and stood up to find out who had dared to disturb such a fine meal.

"Mr. Cooker? Delighted. Eric Canteloube, Landes public prosecutor. May I have a word with you in private? I'll be very brief. I know your time is valuable."

Although he was polite enough, there was something imperious in his manner that irritated Benjamin. No doubt, this representative of the law in a silk suit was used to intimidating people.

"The parlor is at your disposal," Philippe said as he slipped into the kitchen.

The prosecutor took in the room, examining the paintings and photographs attesting to the lineage of the Bouglon family, and then sat in an armchair that swallowed him. He looked like a pale and sickly wren. Benjamin wondered how a man with such a frail physique could have such an overbearing presence. Indeed, sitting in the oversized chair, a pigskin briefcase propped in his lap, he seemed quite satisfied with the power his position conferred on him.

Philippe de Bouglon popped his head through another door, a bit like a scene from a comedy. "Can I offer you a Prada Armagnac, gentlemen?" Philippe asked.

The prosecutor declined the offer as if it were an indecent proposal. Benjamin, on the other hand, cheerfully told his friend, "Break open your 1983. That's a winner if ever there was one."

The winemaker noticed the reproving look on the prosecutor's face. The man wasted no time as he launched into the reason for his visit. The Castayrac affair was about to be settled once and for all. He admitted that it had taken him awhile to believe that Jean-Charles de Castayrac was a criminal who had acted with premeditation. He thanked the famed winemaker for his investigation, which had implicated the baron. Benjamin was tempted to point out that it was Virgile who had discovered the evidence that conclusively refuted the accidental-fire theory. But he didn't interrupt the prosecutor. The man was loquacious and confident. Finally, speaking in a hushed tone, the prosecutor divulged what he considered a secret.

"Imagine, Mr. Cooker. Castayrac went so far as to accuse his own son!"

"Which one?" Benjamin asked.

"Alban, of course! The president of the APC."

The old man, according to Canteloube, harbored a profound hatred for his older son. The baron had accused Alban of masterminding the fire in order to hasten his bankruptcy and foreclosure.

As the prosecutor spoke, he became increasingly passionate and finally leaped from his chair.

"A bit of 1983 Prada, Mr. Canteloube? Frankly, you're denying yourself one the best eau-de-vies in Bas-Armagnac. And offending our host!"

"One drop, then," the prosecutor replied, indicating with his thumb and index finger that he wanted only a little bit.

"I agree that the son doesn't seem to be as white as the driven snow," Benjamin said, pouring more Armagnac in his tulip glass after serving the prosecutor.

"He's ambitious, I'll gladly concede. Even an opportunist. I suspect he's more devious than his father. But he wasn't in Gascony on December 24th. He has an alibi, rather shameful but indisputable. We checked."

"Meaning?" Benjamin asked. Now he was curious.

"On December 23rd and 24th, Alban de Castayrac was at Fauchon Paris promoting Nadaillac Armagnac. Accompanying him on this trip was his devoted colleague, who is also his mistress, a woman named Sylvaine Malric. An employee at Fauchon confirmed the presence of both of them and witnessed some very affectionate exchanges between the two."

The prosecutor was smiling for the first time. His coy attitude only added to the humor Benjamin found in his haughty demeanor and affected presentation. It was even more comical than the tales of Lord Castayrac's shenanigans that Philippe and Beatrice had shared just a short time earlier.

"You see, Mr. Cooker, it's all clear now—"

A knock at the double doors interrupted the prosecutor. Before Benjamin could respond, Virgile was in the room. He looked upset. "Excuse me, boss, but I'm running back to the Cantarels' place," he said. "Joachim's grandfather just had a heart attack. He's hanging on by a thread."

"Go on ahead, my boy. I'll join you momentarily!"

Virgile's announcement put an end to the prosecutor's narrative. The ascetic hadn't even sampled the 1983 Prada. Benjamin concluded definitively that the man wasn't worthy of his esteem. And therefore, his judgments were suspect.

§ § §

When the winemaker arrived at the Cantarel home, Evelyne's eyes were red, and she had her arms around her son. Edmond, her father, was gone. He had died in a matter of minutes—just enough time for the old woodcock hunter to ease his conscience and depart the world in peace.

"No, it's not possible that Castayrac set fire to his wine cellar to collect the insurance money," Edmond had said. "He downgraded his policy a month before the fire, and he knew he was under-insured. I warned him that this was a very risky move. He said, 'My dear Cantarel, my finances will not allow me to pay more. Let's just hope that nothing happens.'"

Already, the priest had appeared, and neighbors were beginning to stream through the door. Following tradition, they covered the mirrors and stopped the grandfather clock's pendulum. They had to start preparing the body for burial right away. Edmond's old spaniel kept scratching at the door. Sensing that the dog was already missing his master, Benjamin let him in and allowed him to settle at his feet.

12

In the countryside of Gascony, far from the big cities where funeral services and burials were efficient and often cookie-cutter, traditions and rites for the departed were immutable. The funeral Mass was always celebrated with incense, prayers, and holy water. Granted, the wake no longer lasted all day and all night, but friends and neighbors paid their respects at the home of the deceased. It was expected, Philippe de Bouglon said as he put his hat back on after leaving the Cantarels' home.

Certainly, Benjamin wasn't at the Cantarels because it was expected. He understood that this was a grievous loss for a warm and simple family. Without Edmond, Evelyne would have had a much harder time raising Joachim. He had been a generous and attentive substitute father to the boy. Now Joachim's teammates were beginning to shuffle in, giving their friend clumsy hugs and pats on the back.

Edmond Cantarel's funeral was scheduled for ten o'clock in the morning. Naturally, the entire town of Labastide would crowd into the church.

Since 1967, he had insured half the residents of this community, and according to everyone, he was a good man who conducted himself with honesty and integrity. It was custom here not to speak ill of the dead. But nobody would have said anything bad about Edmond Cantarel anyway. His only enemies were the woodcocks.

With the Cantarel house full of people, Benjamin took Virgile aside.

"My boy, your friend is in good hands here. What do you say we make another visit to Blanzac?"

"Why's that, boss?"

"Castayrac could not have set fire to his reserves, the old man said. But somebody did. Let's go see what we overlooked."

Château Blanzac was only a mile and a half from the village, and they traversed it quickly, as the weather was windy and wet. Benjamin recognized René Dardolive, the distiller, coming from Domaine de La Coste. He waved to him. René responded with a rather silly smile.

When they arrived at Blanzac, Benjamin and Virgile were soaked. Athos, Porthos, and Aramis undertook to stir the sole occupant of the grounds, but no one came to the door. The courtyard was muddy, and the hood of the DS 19 was raised, making the front of the car look like a gaping mouth ready to swallow anyone who approached.

Benjamin raised the knocker and tapped the door lightly. In vain. Evidently, Blanzac had been given over to the elements. Some of the windows were broken. Others were wide open, and their shutters were banging in the wind. Benjamin and Virgile were looking at each other and wondering what to do when they heard a thud inside the house. Virgile pushed on the door. It didn't resist. They hurried into the vestibule, and Benjamin searched for the light switch to dispel the shadows.

"Shit! No light!" Benjamin cursed.

Virgile motioned to Benjamin to follow him. He clicked on his lighter to see where he was going. But before the winemaker could take even a step, he felt something jabbing his lower back. Was it the barrel of a rifle?

"Don't move, you looters! Don't move, I said, or I'll shoot you like rabbits!"

Benjamin recognized Valmont's voice. He tried to turn around and give an explanation, but a bullet rang out and lodged in the eye of Jean-Sébastien de Castayrac, whose mediocre and charmless portrait adorned the hallway. The painting fell from the wall and broke apart at Benjamin's feet. The winemaker began to pick up the gilded wood frame; immediately a second salvo confirmed the young Castayrac's resolve.

Benjamin looked up from the portrait, and in his peripheral vision he saw a flickering light. Was it a candle? A flashlight? A lighter? A third shot exploded a demijohn, which immediately sent its eau-de-vie spreading across the floor. Realizing what Valmont planned to do next, Benjamin did an about-face and grabbed the barrel of the gun. Looking him in the eye, Benjamin disarmed the pyromaniac assailant. Virgile wasted no time and threw himself on the young Castayrac. He punched him twice, knocking Valmont unconscious.

"You're going at it a bit too hard, Virgile," Benjamin said, feeling how badly out of shape he was.

"Too hard? I didn't intend to let myself get roasted by a lunatic! And while I'm on the subject, I'm grateful that you managed to get that gun away from him, but you were taking an awfully big chance, wouldn't you say?"

"Yes, I have to agree with you, Virgile," Benjamin said, laboring to catch his breath. "Let's not tell Elisabeth about this. In any case, Valmont de Castayrac has just signed his own indictment."

The unconscious man looked entirely peaceful, despite the trickle of blood running from his nose. His shoulders rose and fell with each breath. After tying him up with wire from the garage, Virgile looked for the bathroom and came back with a wet washcloth. He carefully wiped Valmont's face. Then he carried him to a couch in the library, where he slowly came to.

Benjamin Cooker shut all the open windows and closed the shutters over the broken ones. The wind had not abated, and the rain was causing the gutters to keen. Then he started feeding vine stalks and wood into the fireplace. They needed some warmth. As he did at Grangebelle, he placed two bundles of vine stalks and three blocks of oak on the andirons. Virgile was about to light the vines with Valmont's lighter, a Winchester model from the nineteen forties, when Benjamin stopped him.

"Incriminating evidence, Virgile. You would make a very poor police officer."

"Well, I don't think you'll be recruited by any SWAT team in the near future. You could use a workout or two."

The winemaker smiled. "A word of advice, Virgile: don't ever change. Never take yourself too seriously."

Then, as if he owned the place, he walked to the other end of the library and went down the steps to the private reserve where the baron kept his oldest bottles. He rummaged around and unearthed a vial that was perfectly caramel in color. Written on the label in careful calligraphy:

1964
First blending made by
Francisco Vasquez
Cellar master at Château Blanzac
LABASTIDE-D'ARMAGNAC

The winemaker went into the kitchen and came back with two mismatched glasses. He poured a generous serving in each of the two goblets. Benjamin and Virgile raised their glasses and sipped.

"I don't know, boss," Virgile said, giving Valmont a worried look. "I think I may have hit him too hard."

Benjamin walked over to their bound assailant and held his glass under his nose. A second later, Valmont opened his eyes.

"So, young man, do you have anything to say in your defense?" Benjamin asked, using an ember to light his Cohiba.

The last son of the long line of Gascony aristocrats looked nothing like a dangerous aggressor, but rather like a boy who was unnerved and deeply humiliated by the blood flowing through his veins. Benjamin thought it must have been the years of crying that had taken all the color from his eyes. The winemaker and Virgile fell silent and listened to his monologue, interrupted from time to time by the crackling of the oak log in the fireplace.

"I know, Mr. Cooker, that I will never find favor in the eyes of the law. You'd have to live at Blanzac to understand what can push a person to dire measures. A father who ignores you and spends money that he doesn't have anymore. A brother who hates you as if you were not related.

Ruin, bankruptcy, disrepute. I knew Blanzac was going to be sold. The bank had already talking about repossessing. My father had threatened to commit suicide many times in front of me. So, on Christmas Eve, I decided to burn down the wine cellar. It was the only way to save Blanzac. With the money from the insurance, we could have salvaged the Castayrac honor. It was a matter of life and death, Mr. Cooker. Do you understand?"

Benjamin remained silent. He had put down Francisco's Armagnac to give Valmont his full attention. Virgile had stretched out on one of the library rugs and was tracing the design with his fingers.

"Only Francisco would have known that I was the one who was setting the cellar on fire. So I closed the door and locked it, and I went into the Fatsillières Forest and threw the key into the pond, near the roadside cross. Then I watched the cellar burn. Not a long time—just until I called the fire department."

The oak logs were nearly consumed, and the fire was no longer warming Virgile's back. He threw the remaining contents of his glass of Armagnac on the embers, and the hearth was momentarily engulfed in flames.

"I didn't hear Francisco scream. And then there was a series of explosions. Yes, I think I did hear a scream. Just one."

Valmont de Castayrac was no longer crying.

Virgile looked at Benjamin, who nodded. Benjamin handed his glass of Armagnac to his assistant. Virgile swallowed it in one gulp and stood up to release his hostage from the wire that was cutting into his wrists.

"Listen, Valmont, you need to know something: the person you killed in that fire wasn't just your cellar master."

Virgile couldn't find the words. His throat was dry, his voice lifeless. Unable to endure it any longer, Benjamin walked over to his assistant and put his hand on his shoulder. "Tell the boy. You're the one who needs to do it."

So, looking straight into Valmont's eyes, Virgile said the unspeakable.

"He was your father."

His face haggard, the younger son of Elise Riquet de Lauze, wife of Lord Castayrac, didn't raise a word of objection.

He stared at them, his eyes blank. "I know."

Nobody spoke for a long while. Then Valmont explained. "Last week, right before the police came to arrest father—I mean Castayrac— Joachim Cantarel showed up with a rifle, yelling that he was going to kill his father's murderer. In a rage, Joachim had spit out his mother's confession: she had been involved in a crazy love affair with Francisco while he was sleeping with my Elise Riquet de Lauze."

Valmont looked out the window. "Want to know his exact words? 'Even though Francisco had already knocked up your whore of a mother! When your mother found out that her valiant cellar master had switched beds for a girl more in keeping with his class, that was too much humiliation. When you were born, she threw my mother out without a penny of compensation! The man you called your father your whole life—a first-class cheater and a cuckold himself a hundred times over—didn't lift a finger. Let's talk about the Castayrac honor!' Those were his words."

If Edmond Cantarel's rifle hadn't jammed, Joachim would have killed his half-brother.

Valmont stared fixedly at Virgile. He seemed to expect neither pity nor forgiveness. The steeliness of his eyes could have been interpreted as a challenge. Actually, it mirrored one of his mother's favorite sayings: "The eyes of a Castayrac, in order to shine, must be dry." He had been too sad for most of his life to follow that advice.

Breaking the silence, which had become untenable, Benjamin picked up the bottle of 1964 Armagnac, pulled off the cork with his teeth, filled his glass to the top, and handed it to Francisco Vasquez's son, who emptied it without wincing. The boy wiped his lips on the back of his sleeve and flashed a proud smile redolent of fresh nuts and candied plum.

"Let's get it over with, Mr. Cooker. Call the police."

EPILOGUE

Virgile remained in Labastide-d'Armagnac. He had promised Joachim that he would be his most fervent supporter in the match against Hagetmau. He would be in the Cazaubon stands, yelling, screaming, and generally cheering on his new friend. "You'll bring me luck," Francisco's son had told him this with so much emotion, Virgile wouldn't have dreamed of letting him down.

At each attempted conversion, the striker with the amazing kick looked into the bleachers for his friend's approval. Virgile would give Joachim a thumbs-up, and his friend would return it. Sitting at Virgile's right, Constance was elated. When the final whistle blew, she hugged Virgile. They remained in a momentary embrace while the architect of the Cazaubon victory was congratulated by his teammates. A reporter from *Midi Olympique* photographed Joachim smiling triumphantly as he threw his jersey into the delirious crowd. The final score: 39 to 12.

Joachim Cantarel's future as an athlete looked promising. Indeed, the presidents of some regional clubs were waiting for him outside the locker room. Joachim ignored them and rushed into the arms of Constance and Virgile. His happiness was theirs. "*Victorioso! Victorioso!*" he yelled in Spanish, feverishly kissing the medal hanging from his neck—a silver one that Francisco had brought back from a pilgrimage to Lourdes. Joachim was only seven at the time. Looking curiously at the medal, he had asked his mother, "Who's she?" "That's Mary, the mother of God," Evelyne Cantarel had answered. "And me: you are my mother, but who is my father?" the little boy had asked. Francisco had smiled and raced to the river with his lover and son, playfully splashing them when they finally got there.

§ § §

Baron Jean-Charles de Castayrac was sentenced to four years in prison for insurance and tax fraud. After his release, he never returned to Labastide-d'Armaganac. Some said he had gone to Biarritz, where an old lover, recently widowed, had taken him in. Others, however, said the woman wasn't widowed at all. She was merely separated, and her angry husband had shown up one night and shot the baron dead. Whether Castayrac was alive or not, no one seemed to care.

Valmont de Castayrac appeared in Landes criminal court. The nine jurors acknowledged mitigating circumstances but still recommended a sentence of twelve years. He would be eligible for parole after serving seven years.

Shortly after his transfer to the central penitentiary in Seysses, Valmont received a letter from Joachim Cantarel. The Toulouse rugby team's new recruit announced his impending selection for the national team, which would soon compete in the Six Nations Tournament. He promised Valmont a visit in the very near future and told him the DS was safely parked in his garage, covered with a sheet. "It awaits your release," he said before closing his letter with "warm brotherly regards."

Thank you for reading Flambé in Armagnac.

We invite you to share your thoughts and reactions on your favorite social media and retail platforms.

We appreciate your support.

THE WINEMAKER DETECTIVE SERIES

A total epicurean immersion in French countryside and gourmet attitude with two expert winemakers turned amateur sleuths gumshoeing around wine country. The following titles are currently available in English.

Treachery in Bordeaux
Barrels at the prestigious grand cru Moniales Haut-Brion wine estate in Bordeaux have been contaminated. Is it negligence or sabotage? Cooker and his assistant Virgile Lanssien search the city and the vineyards for answers, giving readers and inside view of this famous wine region.
www.treacheryinbordeaux.com

Grand Cru Heist
After Benjamin Cooker's world gets turned upside down one night in Paris, he retreats to the region around Tours to recover. There, he and his assistant Virgile turn PI to solve two murders and very particular heist. Who stole those bottles of grand cru classé?
www.grandcruheist.com

Nightmare in Burgundy
The Winemaker Detective leaves his native Bordeaux for a dream wine tasting trip to Burgundy that turns into a troubling nightmare when he stumbles upon a mystery revolving around messages from another era. What do they mean? What dark secrets from the deep past are haunting the Clos de Vougeot?

www.nightmareinburgundy.com

Deadly Tasting
In a new Winemaker Detective adventure, a serial killer stalks Bordeaux. To understand the wine-related symbolism, the local police call on the famous wine critic Benjamin Cooker. The investigation leads them to the dark hours of France's history, as the mystery thickens among the once-peaceful vineyards of Pomerol.

www.deadlytasting.com

Cognac Conspiracies
The heirs to one of the oldest Cognac estates in France face a hostile takeover by foreign investors. Renowned wine expert Benjamin Cooker is called in to audit the books. In what he thought was a sleepy provincial town, he and his assistant Virgile have their loyalties tested.

www.cognacconspiracies.com

Mayhem in Margaux

Summer brings the Winemaker Detective's daughter to Bordeaux, along with a heatwave. Local vintners are on edge, But Benjamin Cooker is focused on solving a mystery that touches him very personally. Along the way he finds out more than he'd like to know about the makings of a grand cru classé wine.

www.mayheminmargaux.com

ABOUT THE AUTHORS

Noël Balen (left) and Jean-Pierre Alaux (right).
(©David Nakache)

Jean-Pierre Alaux and **Noël Balen** came up with the Winemaker Detective over a glass of wine, of course. Jean-Pierre Alaux is a magazine, radio, and television journalist when he is not writing novels in southwestern France. He is a genuine wine and food lover, and won the Antonin Carême prize for his cookbook *La Truffe sur le Soufflé*, which he wrote with the chef Alexis Pélissou. He is the grandson of a winemaker and exhibits a real passion for wine and winemaking. For him, there is no greater common denominator than wine. Coauthor of the series Noël Balen lives in Paris, where he shares his time between writing, making records, and lecturing on music. He plays bass, is a music critic, and has authored a number of books about musicians, in addition to his novel and short-story writing.

ABOUT THE TRANSLATOR

Sally Pane studied French at State University of New York Oswego and the Sorbonne before receiving her master's degree in French literature from the University of Colorado, where she wrote *Camus and the Americas: A Thematic Analysis of Three Works Based on His Journaux de Voyage.* Her career includes more than twenty years of translating and teaching French and Italian at Berlitz. She has worked in scientific, legal, and literary translation; her literary translations include several books in the Winemaker Detective series. In addition to her passion for French, she has studied Italian at the University of Colorado in Boulder, in Rome and in Siena. She lives in Boulder, Colorado, with her husband.

DISCOVER MORE BOOKS FROM

LE FRENCH BOOK
www.lefrenchbook.com

Shadow Ritual
by Éric Giacometti and Jacques Ravenne

www.shadowritual.com

The Collector
by Anne-Laure Thiéblemont

www.marionspicer.com

The Paris Homicide series
by Frédérique Molay

www.parishomicide.com

The Paris Lawyer
by Sylvie Granotier

www.theparislawyer.com

The Greenland Breach
by Bernard Besson

www.thegreenlandbreach.com

The Consortium thrillers
by David Khara

www.theconsortiumthrillers.com

CPSIA information can be obtained
at www.ICGtesting.com
Printed in the USA
LVOW04*1609050116
469267LV00012B/71/P